Mrs Johnson's Psy

Christopher An.

Copyright 2020 Christop.

This book is dedicated with much love to Glenda and Pam.

Kindle Edition

Table of Contents   2

Chapter 1. The Prologue

Friday 24th December 2021, Nutting Hill, Londinium

Once upon a time, just after dawn on the Eve of Christmas, Mrs Johnson awoke with a start. She peeped her head out over her eiderdown, pulled off her nightcap, removed her ear plugs and her dental guard, took off her eye mask, rose and quickly dressed.

J (as she is known to her friends) is of average height, has one green and one blue plait and a clear and pale complexion. Today, she is sporting tweed waist high trousers and an apricot roll neck pullover. She is wearing fresh daisies in her hair and a silver chain with a large "Om" pendant hanging from it.

J has been living in a small flat just off Portlebelle Road in Nutting Hill since 1979 when at the tender age of 18, she moved from Millington, an historic town situated on an estuary in Humbleshire. Over the years, she has written, performed in a band, dabbled in various forms of retail, read the Tarot, worked in an ironmongers, taken in washing and ironing and further dabbled in various other ventures, collective and otherwise.

"Invite them, invite them all", a deep voice whispered from outside J's bedroom window. "It is time and only you can do this".

J walked over to the window and rubbed off the ice from the inside. She looked out then opened the window.

"Good morning Mr Lovegrove. I thought you had deserted me. You had better come in".

"I am very busy Mrs Johnson and do not have the time to take on human form this morning. The moment has come to gather them together again".

"I'm trying to hold down three jobs Mr Lovegrove. I'm not even bringing in enough money to heat this place. The fridge is empty, all my tights are laddered, I'm living on Farley's Rusks and am three months behind on the rent. I just don't have the time or the energy. Since The Nimbus Pandemic, I've been on my knees".

"On Friday 15th July next year, you will throw a dinner party here and they must all come. All of them, otherwise the spell will be broken forever".

"Who do you mean exactly?"

"I don't have time to explain. As I said before, I am very busy. You know who they are. You know that it must be The Six".

The window slammed shut and J felt a shudder down her spine.

J knew Mr Lovegrove was right and that only she could make this happen. She went to her armoire, fetched out her favourite navy blue pencil case (she had six), selected a recently sharpened 4H and opened her notebook.

Chewing nonchalantly on a rusk, she started a list:

Tdlz
Bog
CC (Christopher Charles)
CA (Christopher Anthony)

Joycie

"That's five", she muttered. "Who can the sixth be? There were only ever five. Cripes! The sixth would be me!"

J looked at her watch and realised she was in danger of being late for her morning job just up the road, making sandwiches at Betsit's Bakery. She made a mental note to procure some invitations from Poundland on the way home, dressed and left for work.

There was an envelope waiting on the hall stand with the letter "J" written on it in blood red.

Inside was a piece of paper, with the following words scrawled on it, also in blood red:

"It has to be psychedelic. Six must become one".

A small clay tablet fell from the envelope.

J turned white as a sheet and gasped for breath.

"Lawks! The double six magic square has returned to me".

Chapter 2. Tdlz

Tuesday 28th December 2021, Millington Lodge, Millington, Humbleshire

"Susan, please dust every single nick nack today and shampoo all the carpets. Peter, the pool please, there were twelve leaves in it last time I looked. Maureen, Glynnis and I will have lobster bisque, three slices of granary toast without crust and a peeled papaya each at exactly 1930. We're busy, busy, busy today. Tennis at 1115, Ladies Munch and Mingle at 1300, cranial massage at 1530, gong meditation at 1630. A busy Millington is a happy Millington!"

Tdlz Gdlpz-Goldfellow and her partner Glynnis have been together for over 30 years. Tdlz is four foot six in height, her head shaved and somewhat over her fighting weight. (She was an internationally renowned featherweight boxer in The Eighties). Tdlz is a slave to fashion and sports a monocle.

Glynnis and Tdlz met in 1985 at a convention for jigsaw puzzle enthusiasts in Rhyl.

When Tdlz retired from boxing in 2001, she had amassed a vast fortune so she and Glynnis moved to the lap of luxury at Millington Lodge, a former home of Barbara Cartland.

"Please miss".

"Yes Susan".

"There's a letter for you".

"Pass me my emerald encrusted solid platinum letter opener".

"Yes miss".

"Oh my goodness. Maurice, my diary please. July 15th next year. Block out the 14th to the 17th. Book a suite for four at The Laslett in Nutting Hill from the 14th to the 16th. Book me a full detox and colonic on the 17th. We'll need Parker and the silver Rolls Royce Phantom with bar fully stocked. Glynnis will remain here".

"Consider it done Miss".

"You are all darlings. Take the rest of the day off".

They bowed and curtsied, walking backwards out of Tdlz' cavernous study.

"Damn I love being rich".

Tdlz stretched out on the chaise longue in her yellow crimplene pantsuit and smiled.

"Mrs Glynnis Gdlpz-Goldfellow come hither, let's push the boat out and have a Drambuie".

Chapter 3. Bog

Wednesday 29th December 2021, Fartlebrook, Humbleshire

"Vladdie, I have a letter from Londinium. Who can it be from? I am intrigued beyond belief. I am tingling with excitement from head to foot. I am a woman possessed Vladimir and by that I mean I am utterly consumed at the thought of what wonderment may be contained therein".

Bog (given name Louise) and her husband Vlad had been living in a small Humbleshire village, Fartlebrook for the last 40 years. Bog is six foot two, slim, blond with not a hint of grey and is very, very posh. She is both flute teacher and costume designer.

Vladimir is a horse whisperer by day and a stargazer by night. He and Bog became pen friends in 1979 when Vladimir was still living in Romania. Bog (being a fellow equine enthusiast) responded to a small ad in "Boots and Saddles" magazine. They fell in love, Vladimir moved to the U.K, and they married in 1980.

Bog's formative years were spent living in Millington, about 15 miles from Fartlebrook. In those days, Mr and Mrs Gdlpz (a Polish/French couple) and their daughter Tdlz lived on one side and on the other Mrs Cartland and her daughter Joycie.

"Vladdie, the letter is from J. After fifteen years of silence, can you believe it? She has invited me to luncheon next July. Says The Six must gather. How jolly peculiar. I shall go. I feel it from deep within my plunging breasts".

"You must darlink. It vill be very super dooper. Please to pass me my ridink boots sveetyheart. I must to whisper.

"I buffed them for you last night Vladdie. The equine community is eager for you. I know it because I feel it".

"You are my Alpha Canis Majoris".

"I need to be sure that Jonas Johnson is out of the picture. All those years ago, I told J that 21 was too young to marry. All those comings and goings over the years since just wasn't right. Mummy and Daddy both agreed. J should have divorced him".

"Draga mea, it vill be magical".

"Vladdie, you're my rock. I shall to Londinium with my flute".

Chapter 4. Christopher Charles (CC)

Friday 31st December 2021, Gussette-on-Spey, Abercrombieshire

CC peered into the bathroom mirror in his boutique Cairngorm croft, a tower of a man at six feet nine with black, shoulder length hair and chiselled features. He and his partner of nearly 45 years, Kelvin MacQuim met at The Highland Games in 1977 when CC was holidaying with his parents in Scotland. CC had been in the year above J, CA, Tdlz, Bog and Joycie at Brocklington Sixth Form College.

CC worked for NASA during the Eighties and Nineties and just into the Nougthies. Nobody knows exactly what he did so there has always been an air of mystery about him. He definitely didn't make it to the moon but has a lovely picture in his living room of him warmly embracing Ronald Reagan.

Kelvin also worked at NASA and beside the picture of CC and Ronnie is one of Kelvin and Nancy.

"Am I not still gorgeous hen?"

"That you are Christopher Charles".

"Och Kelvie, will you look at the lines".

"I'll skelp yer wee behind Christopher Charles if you carry on wi that haver".

CC and Kelvin had recently returned from a "camping" trip across the south of England in their lilac Mini Cooper to research a possible move down South. They eventually decided not to take a tent, opting instead for a comprehensive wardrobe change on each of the 25 days they were away. They stayed in five star Chihuahua friendly hotels as CC and his familiar, Lasher were inseparable.

CC and Kelvin repaired to the kitchen and as they sipped their vanilla lattes, they both heard a soft plop.

"Och Lasher, you're a wee scunner. Kelvie hen, would you administer J Cloth on plop pretty please?"

"It's nae Lasher pet, that there were the sound of Poundland paper landing on hessian".

"Kelvie, we've had no post since 2019. It canna be".

Kelvin raced over to their recently refurbished vestibule and picked up a small manilla envelope.

"It's addressed to you hen".

"Och Kelvie, will you open it, I'm all of a quiver".

"I will not Christopher Charles".

Kelvin passed CC the envelope. He poured himself a generous Bacardi and Coke and tore it open.

CC turned a whiter shade of pale and shrieked:

"Kelvie, it's an invite from J. The Six have to meet. I canna, I canna". I'm coming over all swoony pet".

Kelvin fetched the smelling salts as CC crumpled to the floor.

"You have to Christopher Charles, do it for Lasher and your Kelvie. Man up".

CC rose to his full height of six foot nine, puffed out his manly chest and looked Kelvin in the eye.

"I'll go because I am indeed your man Kelvin MacQuim. We are both men and I shall always stand by you".

"You're are my one and only sweetheart Ceecy. You've got me in the mood for Tammy Wynette".

"I'll put on ma best plaid shirt and booties and grab a couple of stetsons. It'll be a Hogmanay like no other. You can twirl me round the bothy all night hen", purred CC.

Chapter 5. Christopher Anthony (CA)

Saturday 1st January 2022, Nutting Hill, Londinium

CA sank back into his black satin sheets in his emperor sized bed, drawing deeply on a joint packed with the purest and sweetest Thai grass.

CA has been living in the house next door to J since 1983, having grown up in Mellingford, a small village near Millington. He enjoyed a successful and lucrative career as an international male escort and was able to retire in 2005 at the age of 44. Since then, he has been dividing his time between Londinium and The Green Island. CA is six feet in height, his weight ranging from 200-280 pounds, depending on his social calendar and what he calls "life's little pressures." His choice of wardrobe depends on where he is on his weight cycle but "shabby chic" would be his default. CA describes himself as "Elizabeth Taylor meets Jim Morrison".

"Happy New Year Darling. After more than 40 years, each of these precious nights spent with you feels like the first. I am spent. You are and always will be my favourite next door neighbour. Do you think it's time to go public about our special arrangement?"

"On average CA, it's been a bit of a fumble twice a decade since 1977. I think 'occasional' is something of an overstatement".

"As far as the guys are concerned then, I'm still batting for the boys?"

"Well you did on Tuesday".

"My self-control is work in progress darling J".

"T'was ever thus. I trust you used a prophylactic".

"I used a range. 1: I told him my botty is one way traffic. 2. I told him it would be just oral because I'm moral. 3. I insisted on antifungal mouthwash both before and after".

"Who said romance is dead? Tea tree oil I trust? Still just neighbours to the outside world?"

"Alles klar meine kleine Fuehrerin".

"I'm not sure I feel comfortable with your inference".

"Your extensive vocabulary is a thing of great beauty. How's Speet by the way"?

"I struggle to believe my son will be forty next year. He is well and sends his love. He and his wife Biddy are holidaying in Transylvania".

"How delightful. I hope they get a better outcome than Brad and Janet".

"You're warped".

"So will you please help me to arrange this gathering on July 15th? Pretty please CA".

"We have to do this for the sake of our planet. The alternative is unthinkable. My only condition is that you keep Jonas away".

J looked sternly at CA and rather energetically, fluffed up the pillows.

"Don't worry about Jonas. I'll have a word with Mr Lovegrove".

Chapter 6. Joycie

Monday 3rd January 2022, Millington, Humbleshire

"Clinton it's your turn to cook tonight. I've made three thousand vol-au-vents, forty litres of ice cream and eighteen Black Forest Gateaux today".

Joycie is an impressive woman. She has a generous bust, long red hair, freckled complexion and is of average height. Joycie usually favours a kaftan, sometimes sports a turban and chain smokes.

"Darling, I have been flocking for ten hours solid today. I'm totally whacked".

Clinton is co-owner of a local business, "Flockworld".

Joycie drew hard on a Rothmans, downed her Malibu and pineapple and stamped both feet very hard in quick succession.

"You're not happy are you darling?"

"Clinton Wort, thirty seven years ago, I married you for better or worse, for richer or poorer in Millington church with all our friends and family looking on. I work my fingers to the bone fifty weeks a year with my catering business and have my two weeks in Benidorm when Flockworld closes for the factory fortnight in August. I've been wearing the same winter coat since 1989. I never complain because you, our Sharon, Kevin, Jason and Chardonnay are my life. Clinton, once again, it is your turn to cook tonight. Understood?"

"Yes dear".

"Clinton, I need you to ravish me now in the spare bedroom. You know the drill".

"Yes dear".

Clinton went upstairs, changed into a postman's uniform and walked outside while Joycie changed into a cerise halter neck negligee. After five minutes, he rang the bell.

"Letter for you".

"Oh good morning Mr Postman, how fresh faced you look today. I have just stepped out of the shower and my husband has left for the day. Can I tempt you to some of my freshly baked strawberry shortcake?"

"There really is a letter for you".

"Oh let's not worry about such things Mr Postman. Come into my front parlour".

"No really Joycie. There's a letter here for you. It was caught behind the flap. Must have been there for days".

"I've gone off the boil now. Give me the letter".

Joycie eyed the envelope, sniffed it, held it up to the light then opened it.

"Oh my God Clinty. It's from J.

She's invited me to lunch on July 15th. Talk about forward planning".

"You promised me you would never see that woman or any of those weirdo friends of yours ever again".

"Clinton, I am going and you will not stop me. Do you understand? Now please can we try again? Out you go now. Give me five minutes to get back on the boil".

"Yes dear".

Joycie loosened the bow on her cerise halter neck negligee and re-applied a thick layer of matching lipstick.

"I will have my day in Londinium. I deserve it. It'll be fun. I'm a woman who needs to be naughty".

Chapter 7. Five Go Mad in Millington (Part One)

Saturday 14th October 1978, Rooks Bend, Mellingford, Humbleshire

Sheila put the phone down, ran her hands through her curly locks, poured herself a large gin and tonic and heaved a rather worried sigh.

"What's wrong Shilsy?" her husband Ian quizzed.

"Oh Ink, I'm so worried about CA's 18th birthday party. It's just next week. That was Lady Wothchild, the mother of one of the girls who's coming from Beauville. She made me promise that there'll be no hanky panky and that Jemima will sleep alone in her tent. This party is getting out of hand. I think they're planning to turn the front garden into a camp site".

"We've already had this conversation dear. You know my views. The responsibility is yours and yours alone. In return, I get to keep all my organs and dig holes in the garden where the ley lines meet".

"Nice deal dear. The dog keeps falling into the holes and your organs are becoming an embarrassment. Rooks Bend and its inhabitants are a laughing stock."

Ian left the kitchen and went to the sun lounge to locate his dousing rods and tinker with his latest acquisition: a vintage harmonium with a full pedal board.

Sheila and CA had visited the auction room in Millington back in 1976 and made an impromptu purchase of a pretty little Victorian reed organ. In the following two years, buying, renovating and selling old organs had become Ian's latest obsession. The house was filled with them. Sheila had managed to keep the lounge and kitchen organ-free but it was an ongoing battle of wills. She picked up the phone and called her mother, who lived in Bourneville, a nearby coastal resort.

"He's being impossible Jim. Once again, I am shouldering a major event. Just one week to go and all the food to plan. CA is insisting that there be vast amounts of alcohol and most of them will be under age".

"Well dear, if it's anything like your coming of age debacle, you have reason to be concerned. At least you had it on the roof of Remington Towers so most people couldn't see what you were all getting up to. I found two gin bottles, a torn up packet of cigarette papers and a little pile of brown-ish crumbs the following day AND I saw you on the back of that motorbike. Like mother, like son dear, I say. That said, I think he's turning out well so best let it be. Boys will be boys".

Alice MacLear, known to all as "Jim" had lived in Remington Towers, a large art-deco apartment block since the Forties. Sheila and Ian had also lived there early on in their married life. It is still a landmark in Boscleton, once an affluent suburb of Bourneville.

Sheila put the phone down, poured herself another stiff gin and tonic and had a large swig. All of a sudden, there was a great commotion and five teenagers literally fell into the kitchen on top of each other, convulsing with laughter.

"Hello you five. Dear Tdlz, is it not a little warm for a duffel coat in today's heat? Joycie, how cheesecloth does become you. Louise, how is your dear mother? Will you be

20

coming for your elocution lesson on Wednesday J? You must all miss dear CC now he's at university. Christopher, we need to speak".

"No time today mater, we're off for our picnic at Westover Castle. We're taking the ferry from Seahaven. I trust you have lashings of ginger beer for us on ice and that the hamper is packed and filled. I don't know why but the meals we have on picnics always taste so much nicer than the ones we have indoors. It's such a lovely day. The sea and sky are so blue. There's a rainbow around every corner. Will you drop us off to the ferry in The Wolseley Vanden Plas Princess please mater?" sermonised CA.

Sheila took another glug, fetched the picnic hamper out of the larder and the ginger beers from the fridge. They all squeezed into her sparkling new Wolseley Vanden Plas Princess and headed for Seahaven.

As they jumped out of the car, Sheila took her gin and tonic from the walnut dashboard nook, had a swig and looked piercingly at CA.

"We need to talk when you get home".

With that, Sheila effected a skid three point turn, glass in one hand, a Moore's Menthol, clenched in her lips. She accelerated off into the distance in her recently purchased pride and joy.

"Gosh CA, I've never seen your mother do a wheelie like that before", retorted J. "Come on chaps, let's hotfoot it lest we miss the ferryman".

There was something of an Injan summer that October and all but Tdlz were in shorts. They just made it to the ferry and landed near to the castle entrance, which was at the end of a long gravel spit. They walked around the north side of the castle, where it was quieter and laid out everything for their picnic.

"Gosh CA, your mum does make a fine picnic", sang Joycie. "I love scotch eggs, crisps and sardine sarnies, all washed down with ginger beer. Wake up Tdlz, it's one o'clock in the afternoon".

Tdlz pulled her duffle coat hood coat down, scratched her head and yawned.

"When you grow older, you will be a great cook Joycie", forecast J, "and you will be a world renowned female wrestler Tdlz. Lash one up Boggy I'm feeling more premonitions coming on".

"Why does it always have to be I and by that I mean why do I have to roll all the reefers?"

"Because my darling, CA is ham-fisted, Tdlz is usually asleep, Joycie doesn't put enough in and I prefer to observe. You are the resident expert. Yours are truly an art form my darling".

"Well, if you put it like that...."

It was the most beautiful afternoon with the sea as blue as a cornflower and the sky flecked with fluffy white clouds. The Green Island on the other side of Seahaven Water seemed to be floating in the air. Trees were growing all over it, a little hill rising in the middle. It was mysterious, lonely and beautiful, all at the same time. They lay on their backs, Bog's finely crafted number being passed around.

"Ooh err", gasped J. "I'm getting messages".

"And so to the after dinner entertainment", chuckled CA.

"It's you CA. It's a long way in the future, Monday 12th February 2018 to be exact. You're sitting on a terrace in a beautiful garden in Inja near the sea".

"Sounds lovely," beamed CA. "What's the grub like?"

"Don't be ridiculous. I've lorst me thread. Where was I? You are on an epic journey across South Asia. You are temporarily indisposed due to a knee injury so are starting to write a book. Lord, you're writing these very words. How very queer".

"I'll be a bit long in the tooth to go travelling by then won't I luvvy?"

"You will surprise yourself".

"For God's sake, wake up Tdlz", interjected Bog.

"Good morning mummy, tea please," said Tdlz, rubbing her eyes.

"Heavens above woman, it's the afternoon. Take that bloody coat off," growled Bog.

"I love my duffel coat. My neighbour Humf gave it to me. He got it when he was in The Navy".

"It's clouded over, the picture has gone. Hopefully, it'll all make sense in about forty years' time", purred J.

"Crikey chaps", shrieked Joycie. There are two men wearing masks rowing a boat straight towards us. What are we to do? There can ever never be any escaping from difficulties, ever never. They have to be faced and fought".

"See 'em off Tdlz", roared CA to no avail as she was once again fast asleep.

"Don't wake the baby", whispered J.

"I see no baby. Please tell me you are not with child J".

"I am bun-less, oven-wise".

It was too late. The boat had come to shore by now and one of the men was walking towards them with a bag over his shoulder, looking very menacing. They looked at each other and whimpered in unison.

"To the castle!"

Chapter 8. Mrs Johnson's Psychedelic Gathering (Part One)

Thursday 14th July 2022, Millington Lodge, Millington, Humbleshire

"The Phantom is ready for you miss".

"Thank you Parker. We'll be picking up Mrs Wort first then Mrs Ceausescu in Fartlebrook. Mr MacQuim-Margo will meet us at The Laslett".

"Very good miss".

The engine roared and the tyres crunched on fine gravel as they swept down the long drive leading to Millington Lodge.

"Bye bye my shallot", wept Glynnis, waving her moist hanky. "Please be good".

"Not a chance", purred Tdlz as she prepared herself a G&T and a Malibu and pineapple for Joycie.

When they got to Lawn Gardens, Joycie and half the road were waiting. Parker pulled up the Rolls, Tdlz got out and she and Joycie embraced.

"I am SO excited Tdlz. I can't believe this is happening. A new wardrobe of designer clothes and a makeover. You spoil me".

"Darling, we're going to Londinium. We have to look the part".

They drove off as Joycie's neighbours jostled for prime position and posted pictures of Tdlz Gdlpz-Goldfellow, Millington's First Lady.

"To Fartlebrook Parker".

"Yes milady".

They sped across The Old Forest and in no time arrived in Fartlebrook. Parker drove into the Sandy Balls Mobile Home Community and eased the Phantom into a tight space outside "Boggenvlad", one of the larger homes, complete with paddock and small observatory.

Bog came out, drawing deeply on a Sobrani, her hair pulled back into a bun. She was wearing an original Thirties Germaine Monteil silk dress.

"My darlings. My spleen and heart are singing. This is our time. I shall serenade you all the way with my flute".

Joycie shot Tdlz a look. Tdlz got out and embraced Bog.

"A flute of Bollinger first Bog?"

"You know me too well. The woodwind flute can wait. Vladimir sends huge love. And by that, I mean from every ventricle. Joycie, you look spectacular and by that I mean extraordinarily glamorous".

"Oh thanks ever so Boggy. You look fab too. I feel glamorous. My Chardonnay didn't recognise me. Literally. She blanked me and I said: 'Chardonnay it's mum' and she said: 'My mum doesn't wear heels, a push up bra and stockings' and I said: 'I do Chardonnay. Ask your dad' and

26

she said: 'Mum I don't want to know" and I said: 'Best not darling'. Could I have a top up please Tdlz?"

"Girls, did we all receive the same instructions regarding tomorrow?" asked Tdlz, sipping on her third G&T.

"What's Aywhoaskedyer?" Joycie asked. "I Goggled it and it sounds a bit weird".

"Don't you worry my darling. Vlad and I travelled with Ayahuasca last solstice and it was simply amazing. And by that I mean we literally merged. And I'm not talking penetration. I'm saying we were One".

"Oh Boggy. That sounds brill. I'm game".

"Ditto from me but don't tell Glynnis. Not sure whether CC will be up for it. J is obviously in charge so she will. CA will do anything because he is a degenerate whore".

"Lucky bastard", sniffed Joycie. "Who wants to play I Spy? I Spy with my little eye something beginning with M. It's Malibu. I love my Malibu".

"Top up Joycie?"

"I usually stop after two but this is a special weekend. Have you got a little parasol to go in it Tdlz?"

"No".

The Phantom sped along the M3 and before they knew it, they had passed Chislewick and were approaching Nutting Hill.

"Gosh, we've arrived. Parker just drop us here".

"Yes milady. Will you require me again today?"

"Come back at noon on Sunday. Here's a grand. Go wild".

"I shall procure dainties for Mrs Parker".

The three friends tottered into The Laslett and were shown up to their suite. CC was waiting for them, immaculately dressed in a mauve Dior suit, yellow Vera Wang brogues, black Armani shirt and lilac plaid tie, sipping on a Mojito.

"Good evening ladies. Long time no see. I'm working my way down the cocktail list".

"CC are you up for this Ayahuasca lark?" quizzed Tdlz.

"My Kelvie chose the outfit and said I need to chill and be so I'll be flowing with the go. Hugs please".

It was as if 1978 had been just yesterday. The bond was still there. They all hugged then had a collective fit of the giggles.

Tdlz spotted an envelope on a table with their four names on it. She opened it and inside scrawled in blood red were the following words:

"The Double Six Magic Square is now with J. She has read the numbers and will use them to help prepare the potion. She and CA will keep a vigil tonight as the potion brews. It will be in your soup. Onion I think or maybe Leek. Push the yellow button on the table, watch the film and embrace your destiny. Only The Six can turn things around or the world will end on Tuesday afternoon just after 'Loose Women' has aired".

"This is getting a bit heavy", said Bog. "I never miss 'Loose Women'. Jane MacDonald is my favourite and by that I mean she is a real woman because she comes from the north of England. I'm going to press this yellow button".

A large screen descended from the ceiling, the lights dimmed and the four friends all sat down and watched the film "Koyaanisquatsi" play at very high volume.

The curtains closed and the lights came up.

"Vladimir and I just love that film", oozed Bog. "The title is a Hopi word meaning 'life out of balance' and by that I mean it must be a message as to what lies ahead of us. I feel a deep seated sense of responsibility for the future wellbeing of mankind from within my plunging breasts".

No pressure then", whimpered CC.

Chapter 9. Five Go Mad in Millington (Part Two)

Two ticks later on Saturday 14th October 1978, Westover Castle, Seahaven, Humbleshire

In their haste to effect an escape into the castle, CA tripped over Joycie and pulled her to the ground. She reached out to J, who in turn reached out to Bog and they ended up in a quivering heap.

That just left Tdlz, who awoke with a start. She sprang to her feet, pointed her left hand (in duffel coat pocket) towards the man and growled:

"Drop the bag motherfucker or I'll shoot your bollocks off!"

"Good Lord!" ejaculated Bog. "When that woman wakes up, she sure wakes up. Dormouse to ninja in the blinking of an eye".

"Please miss don't shoot. My name's Julian and this is my brother Sandy. We're on our way to a Cops and Robbers party at The Long Basement Bar in Millington. We had to row ashore as I'm desperate to spend a penny. I have a sack full of goodies for later. The water pistol's just for show".

"Drop the bag and pistol then you can go and relieve yourself over there. I said drop 'em. Now!"

"Ooh I do admire strong women", eulogised Julian. "I'll just pop over there then and relieve myself. No peeping ladies".

"Does that mean I can have a shufti Julian?" quizzed CA eagerly.

"Course you can pet. Grab hold of my sack while you're at it".

"Hell's teeth", hissed Bog. "All I wanted was a chilly afternoon and some random homosexual in a mask tools up in a rowing boat and wrecks everything and by that I mean my day".

CA and Julian disappeared off onto the ramparts. Having saved the day, Tdlz was once again fast asleep in her duffel coat. Sandy strode ashore and removed his mask. He was dressed in black flares with a red neckerchief. A flowery yellow shirt was open to the navel, revealing a hairy, bronzed chest. He had shoulder length curly, blond hair.

"Cor", cooed Joycie, dribbling a little bit. "Tasty!"

Sandy ran his hands through his tousled hair, adjusted his crotch, looked straight at J and in a deep, baritone voice, with a heavy local accent said:

"You 'n' me lady. Now".

Sandy strode off towards a turret and J skipped after him, her emergency clutch bag held tightly to her breast.

"Double drat Boggy. I had my eye on him. Just you and me left standing then. Lash us up one each. They'll probably be gone for ages".

Bog heaved a deep sigh, created two perfect little numbers and they lay down side by side on the sand, blowing smoke rings into the cornflower sky. They lay there motionless in complete silence for what seemed like an eternity. Maybe they lie there still in a parallel universe.

"I could murder a Crunchie", yawned Bog.

"Muchie, wunchie lunchie Crunchie", meandered Joycie.

"Joycie darling, Tdlz usually has a box full of chocolate in her left duffel coat pocket. Would you oblige please"?

"I'm on it Steed".

Joycie rolled Tdlz onto her right side, extracted the box and gently rolled her back.

"Crumpets with butter", mumbled Tdlz.

Joycie poured the contents of the box onto the sand.

"Cor Bog. What a lot of chocolate! Here you are. I'm having a Double Decker".

They both took enormous bites and began to chew.

"Mouthfuls all round then", chirped CA, returning with a beaming Julian.

Bog tried to respond but a surfeit of honeycomb had temporarily glued her jaws together.

"I could toy with a walnut whip if there's one going", purred Julian.

"Milky Bar for me please Joycie", chirped CA.

J and Sandy returned, hand in hand.

"I'll have a bag of Maltesers please darling. Alexander, what do you fancy?"

"You babe but I'll settle for a Yorkie".

"What a man", drooled Joycie.

"We've been reading poetry", said J.

"What a waste", muttered Joycie.

"There was a young woman from Ealing..." CA commenced.

"Desist!" growled Bog. "My day is in tatters".

"Tennyson actually", trilled J.

"You'd make a lovely Lady of Shallot", intervened CA.

"Youm brainy folks", mumbled Sandy. "Down my village, men don't do no portry. Moi brother now, he different since he went to the smoke. I bin wi im to they fancy drinking places in So Ho Ho. It's all smoke and dark corners wi men fumblin each uther. I loves im still tho no gentilman will get to lift moi shurt".

"Isn't he a darling?" warbled J. "Now then, we're all going with these two in their boat to Millington Quay. We can pop back to your gaffs in Bath Place to decide who is a cop and who is a robber, do outfits, have a quick one at 'The Ships' then hotfoot it to the party. Wakey, wakey Tdlz".

"Hey, what! Give me my chocolate. You've half inched this month's allocation. I usually make each bar last at least three days".

They all got into the boat and Sandy rowed. The sky was bluer than ever, a gentle breeze rippling the water, the warm afternoon sun beaming down.

"When it was raining last Wednesday, I wrote a new song", ventured J. "I shall sing it to you as we cross the water".

"How lovely", said Bog.

Chapter 10. Mrs Johnson's Psychedelic Gathering (Part Two)

Friday 15th July 2022, Nutting Hill, Londinium

J: Do you think the potion is ready CA?

CA: I had a taste an hour ago and am feeling a bit 'One' already.

J: Singular sensation?

CA: Every move that I make.

J: Thank you so much for making the onion bhajis, aloo gobi, veg biriani, raita and the rotis ducks. It's beer, red or white wine to drink. If they're expecting cocktails, they can whistle. They'll be loaded by the time they get here anyway.

CA: I lashed up a few spliffs to help the journey back down.

J: "Lash" has too many negative connotations for me.

CA: So 1982 darling.

J shot him one of her old fashioned looks, adjusted her pince-nez and got up from her brown corduroy beanbag.

J's one bedroom flat had an amply proportioned reception room. She had briefly lived in the cramped studio next door then took on the flat when her friend Nina eloped with a Nepalese window dresser.

The intercom buzzed long and hard.

CA: Ready or not, here they come.

J pressed the "accept" button and went to the inner door to usher them in. She opened the door and CC fell in, Joycie on top of him. They were all wearing the same clothes as the previous day. CC's mauve suit had a number of undeterminable stains, one shoe was not exactly yellow anymore and the tie was long gone. Joycie had somehow managed to remain looking as fresh as she had the previous day. CC and Joycie were followed by Tdlz and Bog who were feverishly engaged in a heated exchange.

T: But surely a guaranteed annual yield with one year access request is a safer option than riding the market? Of course one should maintain a six figure cash float for unexpected eventualities.

B: You are too risk averse my darling and by that I mean you should take more risks. Not risky risks just risks that are worth taking. My Vladimir is a risk taker and we've had some spectacular gains.

J and CA looked at each other and she discreetly whispered into his ear: "Marching Powder".

CC and Joycie got up from the floor, giggling.

CC: There once was a girl from Devizes with titties of different sizes.

J: Amber light. There will be no get out of jail cards handed out tonight. We have important work to do.

CC: One was quite small, really nothing at all and the other won several prizes. Boom, boom!

CA: Thank you Basil.

CC: Don't give me the brush off CA.

J: STOP! Red light! Time to eat.

T: Couldn't eat a thing.

B: I have no hunger. Where once my stomach was, there is now a void, possibly a vacuum.

Joycie: I could eat a horse.

J: You must all eat daal. The Ayahuasca is in it.

CC: The note in the hotel said onion or leek soup.

B: Daal would be darling.

T: Roughage. Yes. Good.

J: Sit.

B: Don't be a Blue Meanie

J broke into a fit of uncontrollable giggles, remembering the language they have shared since their teens. A "Blue Meanie" is a fierce and music hating creature from the Beatles film, "Yellow Submarine".

CC: Can we play "What's in my cupboard" later just like we used to in the summer of 1978?

T: I never understood that game. There was never a cupboard in sight.

CC: That was the whole point. It was aspirational.

CA: I wonder if Bunty Cottage is still standing. Remember Nicky's 18th birthday party in the basement Margo?

CC: I most certainly do Jerry. It was all about the 'rooms.

CA: I saw God that night.

They convulsed into a long group hug.

J: Eat the daal. There are other things for those of you who have not been touring Colombia.

They formed an orderly queue and filled their plates.

Joycie: This daal is amazing. It's sweet.

B: Sour.

T: Spicy.

CC: Salty.

CA: There's a little bit of me in that daal. That may explain the saltiness.

J: Don't be so disgusting.

Tdlz and Bog played with their food but ate the daal. Joycie, CA and CC wolfed plate after plate. J ate modest amounts, ever mindful of maintaining a svelte physique.

Eventually, they all sank into individual beanbags, sharing tales from their college days.

There followed a prolonged period of silence.

B: Divine and by that I mean green. No I seem green.

T: I am a blue loo.

CC: I feel like foo-foo.

Joycie: Beep, I'm a little sports car.

J: Fasten your seatbelts everyone.

CA: Going up. Ground Floor perfumery, stationery and leather goods.

Chapter 11. Bog's Offering (Part One)

Saturday 23rd July 2022, Fartlebrook, Humbleshire

Good evening everyone, this is Bog writing. I have taken time out from my incredibly hectic schedule to fill in a few gaps.

I decided it was time to introduce a more sophisticated feel to this narrative so I have agreed to briefly be a guest writer. I shall, in my own time share with you all what happened on the night of Thursday 14th July 2022.

My real name is Louisa Patricia Susan Margaret-Rose Cornwallis-West and I was born in 1961 in Calcutta. My formative years were spent in Mellingford-on-Sea, where I went to the local Church of England Primary School. People call me Bog as an alternative to Lou. I can't say that I particularly like it as a nickname and by that I mean I would have preferred just to have been called Ouisa or suchlike. Never mind, it's too late now.

Mummy called me Lou sometimes, which was fine as she wasn't intimating any lavatorial connection. Neither mummy nor daddy ever called me Bog. They would have thought it uncouth, having had strong family connections in Inja.

In 1969, we moved to Number Two Bath Place in Millington. I didn't change schools as mummy and daddy both felt continuity of education was paramount. The Gdlpz family lived next door at Number Three. Mr & Mrs Gdlpz had moved there before Tdlz was born. Lech was the son of Polish emigrants and his wife Brigitte was French. Tdlz their daughter, like me was born in 1961 so we soon became friends and played together on the occasions she was let out of her garret room.

Christopher Anthony also grew up in Mellingford and we have known each other since 1971, having been classmates at Mellingford Church of England Primary School. Even then he was a very naughty boy and once got into terrible trouble for lifting the Reverend Ffoliot Powell's robes during catechism. That said, he has a kind heart and has always made me chortle.

We don't really speak about Julian's terrible accident. He and CA had nearly three blissful years together after consummating their relationship on the ramparts of Westover Castle. On July 21st 1981, they were due to celebrate the wedding of Prince Charles and Lady Diana Spencer at a rather dubious hostelry called "The Vauxhall Bellmont" in Earling Park, Londinium. Julian had gone dressed as Lady Di and CA as his prince.

Julian's five metre train got caught in the end carriage door of a District Line train as he was getting out. CA tried in vain to untangle the train from the train. In some strange way, I can understand why CA spent the next twenty years working as a male prostitute. There is no other phrase to describe his highly dubious career choice. He hasn't been able to listen to Dylan's "Blood on the Tracks" since that truly tragic day.

From 1972-1977, CA, Tdlz and I went to Monklands Comprehensive in Millington as mummy and daddy also had a very progressive approach to education.

J moved to Millington in 1973. We also became close friends at Monklands, where many of us started our relationship with mind altering substances. J and I both

41

come from prime stock so it was inevitable that we would bond.

Joycie Cartland and her mother Anna moved into Number One Bath Place in 1977, around the time we all went to Brocklington College to do our A Levels. We Six all spent a lot of time together in Joycie's bedroom, smoking cannabis, listening to Genesis and Pink Floyd. I created a mural of an Alice in Wonderland mushroom on Joycie's bedroom wall, a tribute to the local fayre growing wild in the nearby forests, which we regularly harvested.

Christopher Charles joined our circle of friends at Brocklington College in 1977. He was a year above us and had a yellow Ford Capri that I found rather offensive. He and CA seemed to have a lot in common apart from both being rather vulgar. It only became evident some years later that they were "gentlemen of the piers" if you get my drift. At least Christopher Charles found a respectable partner to settle down with early on.

So there you have it. I trust that I have provided you with a little more background information about our circle of six. I feel that my extra flourish can only add value.

And so to the night of July 14th, when I arrived at The Laslett in Nutting Hill with Tdlz and Joycie. We knew not why we had all been summoned by J other than that it would involve Ayahuasca. My husband Vladimir and I being liberal minded experimentalists had already had an Ayahuasca experience so I was game to journey again.

Ayahuasca for those of you not in the know is a brew made out of the Banisteropsis capi vine and other ingredients. The indigenous people of the Amazon basin use it as a traditional spiritual medicine. It has a powerful effect on the brain's serotonin receptors.

It was exceptionally gracious of Tdlz to have me and Joycie driven to The Laslett. I do enjoy being in a Rolls and I shall confess that I may rather have overindulged in the Bollinger.

To be honest, Tdlz' chosen career as a female wrestler always baffled me but I think it helped to satisfy the inner man in the woman. By that, I am not wishing to sound dismissive or patronising. Vladimir always tells me I am sensitivity personified.

The Laslett is my kind of hotel: top end but low key. Tdlz is well known there and stays regularly when she comes to Londinium for female boxing conventions. She was quite the star for some years. Word must have got out that she was coming. When Parker brought the Rolls to a halt, there was a posse of fans, I think female but it can be difficult to tell. Vladimir tells me I am femininity personified so gender-wise you know where you are with me.

An elegant man took us all up to our suite and Christopher Charles was waiting for us. It must have been nearly 45 years since we had last met and initially I was a little taken back by his appearance. He was still sporting the shoulder length black locks (though surely they were now dyed) and an outfit that I can only describe as Victorian Gothic meets Beckham. By that I am not wishing to sound uncharitable. I am a woman who speaks her mind. Vladimir says I am assertiveness personified.

After we had all embraced, feeling the last forty years falling away like leaves from a deciduous tree, Tdlz read out the message that had been left for us. I have to say, it

43

rather took us all by surprise as we were just expecting a bit of a jolly. Being an existentialist and feeling great responsibility for contributing something of value towards the collective consciousness, the idea of helping to save the planet rather appealed to me. I was however troubled at the prospect of losing my daily fix of "Loose Women". Jane McDonald is my anchor, demonstrably having working class roots but so grounding for a woman such as I.

Perhaps I was a little hasty in pushing the yellow button on the table but I was eager to know more. Vladimir tells me he has never met a more adventurous woman, in every sense.

We were all a little startled when a screen descended from the ceiling in our reception room.

Vladimir and I are both great followers of Godfrey Reggio and Phillip Glass (director and music director "Koyaanisqatsi") so the impact of what was being conveyed was not lost on me.

I determined from that moment that with my trusty flute alongside me that I would fulfil my destiny to save the planet, even if it meant giving up my daily Jane fix.

Chapter 12. Five Go Mad in Millington (Part Three)

Just a bit later still, Saturday 14th October 1978, Millington Quay, Millington, Humbleshire

Sandy pulled the little boat into Millington Quay, his bronzed biceps glistening in the late afternoon sun. Joycie sighed deeply and disembarked, followed by J, Tdlz and Bog. Julian and CA were the last to leave the boat, both looking a rather pale shade of green. They staggered onto the little jetty, clutching two large paper bags.

"Youm landlubbers. Corl yerself a bruther of mine. The waters be flat as the village pond today and you chucks yer guts up all over me rowlocks. That friend of yorn baint be no better. Me flares is all flecked with puke".

Bog looked to the skies and muttered something incomprehensible.

"I'm sorry brother", mewled Sandy. "Promise I'll wipe it all off".

CA started to dab at Sandy's flares with a moistened hanky.

"One inch closer to me tackle and I'll deck yer".

"Righty ho", chirped J. "You two boys wait at 'The Ships'. The five of us will wander up the road to Bath Place, freshen up and arrange outfits".

Bath Place was only about five minutes' walk from Millington Quay. They called in to Number Three first, where Tdlz lived in a two storey fisherman's cottage. Bog lived next door at Number Two, which with Number One

45

was a pair of grander Georgian houses. Tdlz' father Lech was out fishing. As she turned the key in the lock, her mother stood at the door.

Brigitte Gdlpz was obviously in the middle of doing her hair.

"Hello sweetie, hello Chrees and girls, my air is in curlers. I ave just washing it. I look terrible. Sac abominable! Tdlz take off zat rideeculous coat. Your body will be cooking like ze Sunday joint, non?"

"Yes mummy, thank you. Will that be all?"

"My leetle girl, she is very rude to her mummy, non? I will ave to make ze punishments later and smack both her bottoms. Crees, ow is your muzzer?"

"She is well and sends her regards Mrs G. Just a rinse through today or are you going to do your roots?"

"Yes, yes I go to Boot chemeeest later. I ave to go for Lech. His leetle problem is grumbleeng today".

"You're always grumbling mother".

"Oh my leetle girl, she is so funny, non? Come and seet in ze room everyones. I will bring tarte aux pommes".

The house Tdlz had lived in all her life boasted a walk through living and dining area, which Mrs G always referred to as "ze room". On the wall in the living area, was a large photograph of Tdlz sporting a curly perm, sitting outside her grandparents' house in the small village of Cul-de-Vache near the French-Swiss border.

"Mrs G, before you return with your delectable patisseries, could you explain what something means in French if I write it down?" ventured CA.

"Mais oui Crees".

CA handed her a piece of paper with the words "à l'eau, c'est l'heure" written on it. Mrs G read the phrase out, tugged at a stray curler then read it again.. and again.. and again.

"I do not understand eet. I am very confuse".

J and Bog were by now propping themselves up against a rather large cuckoo clock, struggling to control fits of the giggles.

CA kept a straight face and suggested that he thought it was a motto for the French Navy. Mrs G looked even more confused and poked at another stray curler. She walked out of the room and a few minutes later returned, bearing a plate of her freshly baked tarte aux pommes. Mrs G left to put the finishing touches to a mural of a small Alp on the garden wall.

"I'll just pop up to get a stripy top and a bit of rope", said Tdlz.

Tdlz returned a few minutes later, looking a bit more robber like and had substituted the duffel coat for a rather worn Afghan.

"We're off mummy. Thank you. Run for it chaps".

Mrs G was not to be deprived of her farewells and returned with a piano accordion strapped to her chest, a few flecks of paint on her nose.

"How delightful Mrs G," enthused J. "Play us out with 'Chanson du Lac' please?"

"Dear God no. This isn't happening", wailed Tdlz. "See you later mummy".

"You are going to 'Ze Sheepings', non?"

As they left Number Three, Mrs G stood on the doorstep, her arms flailing in the late afternoon breeze as she tried to remember the song.

Chapter 13. Bog's Offering (Part Two)

Monday 25th July 2022, Fartlebrook, Humbleshire

Vladimir and I have just enjoyed a very pleasant few days with most of our close relatives at home: my Aunt Yootha, sisters Crinoline and Praline, their husbands and Praline's children. We had quite the house full. Darling Vladimir cooked guinea fowl, goose and all the trimmings. I had pre-prepared a cold sweets trolley and served the drinks. They all went this morning so I can finish off my offering now while I sipping on my evening glass of Campari.

After we watched the closing section of "Koyaanisqatsi" in our reception room at The Laslett, the screen ascended into the ceiling and Christopher Charles fainted.

Joycie and Tdlz were a tad trembly too and after administering smelling salts to CC, we all had a stiff drink and I called J.

B: Darling, it's been fifteen years and out of the blue comes this invitation to what seems like a reunion. It seems that we're all going to be hallucinating vigilantes and by that I mean I have no problem with that as such being a global philanthropist.

J: Chill Boggy, I've checked out the runes and the numbers on the double six magic square and am confident of a positive outcome.

B: I thought you lost that rather odd relic years ago J. You're talking in riddles. I am feeling very unrelaxed and Vladimir is not here to soothe me and by that I mean my anxiety levels are peaking.

J: Have you been powdering your nose darling? You know it's not chill conducive.

B: Yes, um well, it's all down to Tdlz. One of her fans gave her a bag full of the best Colombian.

J: I suggest you all have an early night, drink plenty of chamomile tea and maybe play a hand of whist. I have to go. CA has been an angel helping me with the food but has gone AWOL. One of his former clients is in town and he has come out of retirement to oblige. He left with little or no warning and took my precious collection of Edgar Allen Poe pomes. I'm stressed, rather tetchy and all of a dither. See you tomorrow. Don't be late.

And with that she hung up, rather angrily I would say. I was blowed if I was staying in. I hardly ever go to Londinium so I wanted my night on the town.

"Right girls (and CC)", I said, "who fancies a large night? Saving the world can wait until tomorrow".

There was consensus in the room that So Ho Ho should be our destination so we all had a freshen up and Tdlz booked a stretch limousine for the night. I decided to take my flute. We had another three or four drinks and hit the road. Joycie was very much the worse for wear by then but managed to rally.

At CC's suggestion, our first stop was Madame Jojo's in Brewling Street. It had had re-opened "for one night only" after many years. Tdlz made a few calls and arranged four tickets at great expense, after calling her old friend Marysia, also known as "The Singing Psychic."

Marysia met us at the door and got us a table right by the stage. She joined us and several drinks later, we had reached the part of the evening where members of the audience were invited to perform. Joycie was the first to put her hand up and screamed at the top of her voice.

"I wanna do a strip. Bog, get your flute out and play us all a song while I get my kit off".

Looking back, it all happened so quickly. Joycie got up onto the stage to a whooping audience and I was right by her side with my flute. Why, oh why, oh why did we let her do it and why, oh why, oh why did I get on the stage next to her, playing my flute along to "The Stripper"?

Just as Joycie had whipped off her bra and was about to remove her undies, Christopher Charles lunged onto the stage in a rather balletic kind of rugby tackle. Joycie grabbed hold of his tie, which ripped into two pieces, went rather pale, vomited all over him, they both fell to the floor and she passed out.

Needless to say, we were all asked to leave so the stretch limousine took us back to The Laslett, where we deposited Joycie in the recovery position, having sent her outfit to be dry cleaned overnight.

"To Heaven", shrieked CC. "Let's boogie the night away ladies at the best club in town!"

So that's what we did. CC spent the whole night on the dance floor, having cleaned his outfit as best as he could. Sadly, Joycie's vomit had rather penetrated one of his shoes, which was now more brown than yellow. I shall confess that Tdlz and I went to powder our noses quite a few times in the ladies lavatories that night but Vladimir is not to be told.

We danced the night away until Heaven closed around 5am.

There was no point going to bed by the time we got back to The Laslett. We dropped Marysia back to her pad in Cheltingsea and joined her for a rather long liquid and powder breakfast.

We got back to The Laslett around noon and Joycie was sitting at the bar, looking immaculate and downing tequila shots.

"You absolute rotters, you dumped me and left me all on my own. I got the last laugh though, I had breakfast with Jane McDonald. She's staying here this weekend. What a lovely woman!"

I cannot tell you how devastated I was. Wonderful night though I had, I would have traded it for just five minutes of Jane's home spun philosophies.

We decided to let Joycie have her moment and to this day have never told her what actually happened that night. I was so hoping that Jane would come back and join us but it wasn't meant to be. I had to satisfy myself with the strains of her most memorable version of "Down Town" playing in the background and by that I mean the definitive version, none of that Petula Clark drivel.

J's flat was five minutes' walk from The Laslett so we had another drink or five, staggered down the street, found her house and pressed hard on the buzzer to her flat.

I am pleased to report that Jane MacDonald and I spent a delightful hour together this afternoon as I reclined in front of "Loose Women". I can only hope that bodes well and by that I mean that the world has not as yet ended.

The rest you know.

Chapter 14. Five Go Mad in Millington (Part Four)

Just after the last bit, very much still Saturday 14th October 1978, Bath Place, Millington, Humbleshire

The door to Number Two Bath Place opened and a tall, rather elegant and immaculately dressed woman stood there, her long hair piled up, a cigarette in the corner of her mouth, whisky glass in hand.

"What in heaven's name is that cacophony...? Oh good afternoon Brigitte, good afternoon you five. Do come in".

Mrs G walked slowly backwards into Number Three and shut the door behind her, several more curlers falling out on the way.

"Look chaps, time marches on", said Joycie. "I'll go and get ready now so come to mine after".

Joycie walked next door and let herself in.

"Do come in my darlings. Come to the kitchen. Who wants a drink?" purred Mrs Susan Cornwallis-West.

"Your mother is SO cool Boggy", whispered CA. "I love your kitchen. Let's go".

"Mummy, we can't stay long. We're going to a party. I need to dress up as a policeman".

"How frightfully delicious my darling. I think I still have Monty's Home Guard uniform in the attic. Would that do?"

"Super mummy and by that I mean perfect".

"Just a tick darling. I'll do a few nips and tucks. Help yourselves my darlings".

They had spent many an afternoon and evening in Bog's kitchen putting the world to rights with Mrs CW. It was one of many homes to them. The large open plan kitchen looked out to an internal patio and the walls were covered with framed prints and a good few originals. The room was rather dominated by an Elizabeth Frink bronze head, known by the family as "Gus". They all helped themselves to wine and beer.

"Lash one up Bog. Let's have a quickie", urged CA.

Bog dutifully carried out her now familiar task and they repaired to the patio. As Mrs CW returned, the phone rang and she answered it.

"Crinoline darling, where are you, we miss you. Right, yes, hang on, I'll get her....LOOOOOUUUUUUUISSSSE!"

"My God, your mother's got a pair of lungs on her!" exclaimed CA.

"Coming mummy".

Bog went to the kitchen and Mrs CW walked out to the patio and sniffed.

"Such a divine smell. Takes me right back to Inja in The Forties".

"Bog's mother is SO cool", enthused CA.

They all returned to the kitchen while Bog finished a conversation with her sister.

"My sister is nuts. Right chaps let's go".

They thanked Bog's mother, who embraced them all as they left, Bog now decked out in Monty's old uniform, several sizes too big. Her mother was a gifted seamstress so had made some swift alterations. They went next door to Number One. Tdlz picked up the doorknocker and let it drop with a loud thud. After a while, the door was opened by Mrs Anna Cartland, a tall, rather stern looking woman in her fifties, short grey hair, ankle length skirt.

"Um, erm. We've come for Joycie", stuttered Tdlz.

"If Diana-Joyce were in, she would have answered the door".

Door slam.

"Gosh that was rather abrupt", sniffed Bog.

A minute or so later, Joycie came to the door.

"I'm so sorry chaps. Mum's glazing a batch of figurines at the moment and she doesn't like being interrupted. Come on in".

They walked to the top of the house into Joycie's bedroom.

"I'm a robber chaps. Loving the outfit Bog. J, what about you and CA?"

"We are undercover detectives from Special Branch", said CA.

"We should go soon", said J. "The boys are waiting at 'The Ships' and will be wondering where we are".

They went downstairs and CA popped his head into the studio Joycie's mother worked from.

"So sorry to have bothered you Mrs C. I hope all is well with you".

Mrs Cartland emerged, smiling.

"Hello dear. I was rather engrossed earlier. Quick G&Ts on your way out?"

"That would be delightful".

"Mum likes you CA. She never smiles at me like that".

"Fetch the glasses Diana, ice, lemon and tonic. Come on girl, quick sticks".

They all repaired to the drawing room. Mrs C sat in her usual place, lit a cigarette and poured a generous amount of gin into each of the six glasses Joycie had brought in. She added a slice of lemon and ice to each one and topped them up with tonic.

"Cheers everyone. Louise, what on earth are you wearing? It looks like a Home Guard uniform. My uncle served you know. They were old men but they helped to keep us safe".

"Have you ever worn a uniform Mrs C? You'd make a super matron", asked CA.

Mrs C raised her left eyebrow and there was a long silence. She looked CA in the eye and they both burst into laughter.

"That was close", whispered Joycie to J. "I don't know how he gets away with it".

"So what are you children up to now, dare I ask?"

"We're going to a party at the Long Basement Bar with two men we met at the castle mum".

"Ye gods girl. Please do not crash through the door in the small hours. You can go now".

"Yes mum".

They finished their drinks and. Mrs C offered a cheek to CA, who pecked it very gently. Then they all left.

"Hip Hip Hooray for The Bath Place Mothers!" shouted J at the top of her voice as they all skipped down the road.

Chapter 15. Six Go Back in Time (Part One)

Easter Sunday 1979, Number Two Bath Place, Mellingford, Humbleshire

"I am completely over-egged thank you", said J as Mrs Susan Cornwallis-West offered her another wedge of chocolate.

"Me too", sighed Joycie, stretching out on the chaise longue in the open plan kitchen. "Mum keeps hassling me to do A Level revision. It's all got rather tedious of late".

"Tell me about it", lamented Tdlz. "Mummy has been locking my bedroom door from the outside for hours at a time".

"I feel like Cecil the worm after he'd eaten all the cabbages in the world", said J. "Where's CA? He's been gone for ages. He can't still be in your bog, Bog".

"I shall go and search for him", sighed Bog.

"It's so good to be back home from uni", said CC. "Did you miss me everyone?"

"We were like a boat short of a rudder", offered J. "Has uni been lark-ish?"

"Och, you have no idea hen. My Kelvie and I are finally together. I canna believe it's nearly two years ago now that we met at the Highland Games. He still holds the record for the under 18 caber tossing category. That day I first saw his rippling muscles, I knew he was the man for me. When he decided to go to the same uni as me, I canna tell you how my heart leapt. We've a lovely little flat together".

"Why are you speaking with a Sottish accent CC?" asked Bog.

"I think it's osmosis," muttered CC somewhat remorsefully.

"Don't listen to my daughter CC. It all sounds delightful", purred Susan. "When I was in Shimla in The Forties, man on man activities were rife but very much a behind closed doors thing. We were all free spirits."

Bog looked to the heavens, left and shortly afterwards returned with CA. He was looking a little green around the gills.

"I've been sick", said CA.

"That's what happens when you eat five cream eggs in a row", growled J. "It's also not a nice way to speak in front of Mrs CW".

"Darlings, I'm unshockable. Would you excuse me please? Crinoline is coming for dinner and I need to pop into town to do a bit of shopping".

Susan Cornwallis-West donned her bottle green cape and feathered hat, picked up her shopping basket and left

"I didn't know your mother had been to Inja Bog", said Tdlz, gently nibbling on a very small piece of chocolate.

"I was born in Calcutta shortly before she and daddy returned to Mellingford. Grandfather Monty was involved with overseeing the construction of the Kalka-Shimla railway line. He was born in Shimla and his father, great-grandfather Rupert had been there since the 1840s. Shimla was the summer capital of British Inja due to its altitude of approximately 2300 metres and by that I mean it was cool and also has spectacular views. Rupert was a very gifted artist. See that picture on the wall over there? Rupert painted that".

There was a long silence after Bog's monologue. Everyone gazed at the picture of a church sat upon a hill with the words "Christ Church (Shimla)" written under it.

"I wish, I wish, I wish that we were all there right now", chanted J, clutching the double six magic square clay tablet she had recently purchased from a man called Mr Lovegrove on Millington Market.

The Six all continued to gaze at the picture as the room darkened. There were swirling lights, all the colours of a rainbow and a mist started to envelop them all. The room started to spin around and it went completely pitch black.

The Six clung on to each other and closed their eyes in terror.

J was the first to open her eyes and let out a cry of amazement.

"It's the church from the picture. Right there at the end of the road".

Three women in rather old fashioned clothing stood in front of them, the middle one staring straight at them.

"Goodness me children, get up off the ground. What would your parents think?"

"Where are we, what year is it?" stuttered Bog.

"Why child, what is troubling you? You are all dressed so peculiarly. I suppose it must be yet another new Shimla fashion. It's 1926 of course, Easter Sunday. Monty, go and get us a table at Ashiana. We'll catch up with you".

"It seems my wish came true", gasped J. "I think that woman might be your grandmother Bog".

Bog had gone rather pale. She stood up, composed herself, looked at the woman in the middle and asked:

"Excuse me for asking ma'am but would you tell us your name? I am Louisa Cornwallis-West and these are my friends Tdlz, CA, J, CC and Joycie".

"I am Sophia Westover and these are my aunts Praline and Crinoline. My husband Monty has gone on ahead. Why do you ask child?"

"Erm, well it's only polite to introduce oneself is it not and by that I mean courteous".

"I suppose so child. It's quite uncanny how you have the look of Monty's mother about you. We are expecting our first. If it's a girl, we'll call her Susan, Charles for a boy. So what brings you to Shimla this Easter Sunday?"

"We're just here for the day", said J. "After that we'll be heading home".

"And where is home child?"

"Dharamshala. Our fathers have all been helping with the rebuilding after the earthquake", fibbed J.

"You have a long journey ahead of you. Are your parents not travelling with you?"

"We're meeting them later. They're with friends nearby. We came to Shimla after we saw a beautiful painting of the church. We wanted to see it in the flesh so to speak".

"Monty's father Rupert was a painter. He only passed away last year. We're selling some of his paintings at the moment to raise money for the church roof. They're on display at Sham Lall & Sons gallery. You should go and have a look. Well, we must be on our way. Enjoy your day".

Sophia Westover and her sisters turned and walked off into the distance.

"That really was my grandmother", gasped Bog. "I'm feeling very strange. Let's go to the church. It might help us to focus on what to do next. Like how we're going to get home, if ever".

Chapter 16. Party Time at Rooks Bend (Part One)

Saturday 21st October 1978, Rooks Bend, Mellingford, Humbleshire

"Good morning Jemima, how lovely to see you. Are you not a little early for the party dear?" asked Sheila, furrowing her brow.

Jemima Wothchild had just hitchhiked from Beauville. She walked up the driveway to Rooks Bend, her tent slung over her shoulder, puffing on a self-rolled cigarette. Jemima is 17 years of age, well above average height but not quite what you would call tall. She prides herself on maintaining her size 8 physique and has long, flowing blonde hair. Jemima has piercing blue eyes and is thought of as something of a local beauty among the men folk of Beauville. Her grandfather, Sir Horace had been surgeon to Edward VIII, who knighted him in his pyjamas from the royal bed with Wallis at his side. Jemima's father, Colpoys had inherited the title after the death of Sir Horace. The Wothchild family reside at Mooning Hill Towers, the family ancestral home in Beauville, Humbleshire.

"Good morning Mrs Rhodes, how jolly lovely to see you on this very fine sunny Humbleshire morning. CA did say to come any time so here I am. Where's the best place to pitch my tent?"

"May I ask dear, is that a one or two man tent?" asked Sheila, taking a gulp from a hip flask.

"It's my jolly snug little one woman tent. Just enough room for me and my camping stove".

"That's a relief dear, erm I mean, how very cosy. Are we expecting many campers?"

"Gosh Mrs Rhodes!" guffawed Jemima. "No more than thirty tents I'd say. Where's CA?"

"Last time I saw him was a week ago, when I dropped everyone off at Seahaven. He called on Monday to say he'd made a new friend called Julian at a party and that he'd been staying with him I know not where. It's all too much. Brocklington College has been calling to ask where he has been. I've had to arrange everything all on my own".

Sheila paled somewhat as a white Triumph Stag, driven by Julian sped up the drive. CA jumped out, his new blond highlights glistening in the warm autumn sunshine.

"Good morning mater. I trust you have everything under control. This is my friend Julian".

Julian got out of the Triumph Stag, decked in black leather from head to foot.

"Such a pleasure to meet you Mrs Rhodes. May I introduce myself: Julian Salisbury".

"I er, I mean um, yes indeed. So you are Julian".

"In the flesh Mrs Rhodes. From my head to my tippy toes".

"I am seeing a lot of black leather Julian but not a lot of flesh".

At that moment, a Volkswagon campervan inched its way up the drive, driven by Sandy with J next to him on the front seat. Bog, Joycie and Tdlz all fell out of the back.

Sandy jumped out of the van, did a little half bow and extended his hand to Sheila.

"Alexander Salisbury ma'am. It's a proper pleasure to make yor akwaintince. I got a hip flask just loike yors".

"Yes, indeed Alexander. Yes indeed. Well children as you have all arrived rather early, I'll take that as a sign that you'll be helping me".

"Of course we will Mrs R," chirped J. "We have just returned from The Green Island. It is a most magical and verdant place. After the party at the Long Basement Bar in Millington, we all hopped into Alexander's campervan and got the first ferry over on Sunday. We thought CA deserved a decent run up to his coming-of-age".

Sheila smiled. She was very fond of J and found herself thinking back to her own coming-of-age party (21 in those days). Her mother Jim had indeed spotted some evidence of a party-fueled night. It is true that she got onto the back of Montgomery Micklewaite's Harley Davidson and had a passion fuelled week in Dawlish.

"Your Noel? Will he be bringing his own tent?"

"Noel? Lordy to goodness no Mrs R, he'll bunk up with me".

Jemima guffawed, tripped over J, fell against the ornamental birdbath, which split into two pieces and ended up flat on her back.

"I'm so sorry Mrs R, I promise we'll just spoon. Let's all relax and have a nice cup of tea. I have a special blend that will soothe you Mrs R", said Jemima, giving the others a sly wink. "The rest of you, help Millington Sail and Tent Company erect the marquee in the garden".

"That sounds like a very good idea Jemima", whimpered Sheila.

Just as they were about to go inside, a yellow Ford Capri glided up the drive. CC and Kelvin MacQuim got out, both in full Highland dress.

"Hello my darlings", cried CC. "Ma Kelvie and I have motored all the way down from Edlingtonburgh to surprise you all. We just couldn't miss the party, could we pet? Mrs Rhodes, this is Kelvin MacQuim, my intended!"

"Come with Mrs R", said Jemima, propping Sheila up as she started to slide to the ground. "I'll fire up my stove. You'll have a nice soothing cuppa in no time".

"I'm not at all familiar with the Quim clan", wheezed Sheila as they eased her into a beanbag on the front lawns.

Chapter 17. Six Go Back in Time (Part Two)

Easter Sunday 1979, The Ridge, Shimla, Himachel Pradesh, Inja

The Six walked towards Christ Church in total silence along The Ridge: a large open space located in the middle of Shimla. They passed Ashiana, a rather grand looking restaurant with a large terrace overlooking Shimla Valley. They could see the three ladies sitting at a window table with a very distinguished looking older man.

"Gosh, that must be Grandfather Monty", whispered Bog. "And by that I mean my mother's father".

They walked a little further and reached Christ Church. There was a big crowd outside, queueing to get in.

"I do love a good hymn", trilled J.

The Six filed in, one at a time and found an empty pew. An Easter Mass was about to begin. CC and CA, both being notorious fidgets started to whisper and giggle. Tdlz fell asleep and started to snore rather loudly.

"Hell's teeth, you three, why don't you go for a walk and meet us outside in an hour?" hissed J.

"Sieg Heil!" exclaimed CA.

CC involuntarily broke wind rather loudly as he stood up and the three of them tiptoed out of the church.

"Shall we go for a wander chaps?" suggested CA.

They walked down some steps and found themselves on The Mall, a smart street lined with quaint shops. After about ten minutes, the crowds lessened as they approached the outskirts of Shimla.

"Shall we share half a Bounty?" chirped Tdlz.

"You're too kind", quipped CA. "I wish we had some of your mother's tarte aux pommes".

"I shall also be a great pudding cook one day", proclaimed Tdlz. "I am planning a new recipe. There will be ginger and custard. Aren't those buildings lovely?"

All of a sudden, CC shrieked: "Will you look up there. It's a sign from ma Kelvie".

A big sign over a large framed wooden gate had the words "Kelvin Grove" on it. On a little sign underneath were the words "Built in 1850, formerly The United Bank of Inja".

"Your Kelvie isn't the only Kelvin in the world you big dollop", said CA.

"Well thank you very much Jerry! I am missing him and feel comforted".

"You're a big girlie Margo".

"Boys, stop it. This is no time for a spat. That building over there is Clarkes Hotel. I need to pay a call. Let's go in", said Tdlz, shuffling somewhat.

The boys sat in the foyer as Tdlz searched for a lavatory. It was rather grand with turbaned men in uniforms at every corner.

"May I be of assistance gentlemen?" asked a turbaned man in uniform.

"No thank you very much, thank you kind turbaned man in uniform", said CC. "We're waiting for our friend".

"As you wish sir".

Tdlz emerged looking a lot happier.

"Did you do a number two?" asked CA. "You look like a weight's lifted".

Tdlz reddened and shot CA a very dirty look.

"We should head back", she said.

They walked back to the church along shady, tree lined roads.

Bog, J and Joycie were waiting outside the church.

"I have been uplifted", sang J.

"Have you purchased a new brassiere hen?" asked CC.

J ignored CC's remark completely and said:

"We must go and see the Viceregal Lodge. We were chatting to a nice gentleman in the church. He's going to arrange a grand tour for us. Then we must go home. Fear ye not my lovelies, I know not how but my guides have been very reassuring".

They walked down The Mall in the opposite direction from the way CC, CA and Tdlz had been and after a while, passed the old railway station on their left.

They followed The Mall, winding up and down and as they approached The Viceregal Lodge, a policeman in full dress uniform approached them.

"Good afternoon, ladies and gentlemen", he said. "We have been expecting you".

"Cor", whispered Joycie. "He's very handsome. I'd buff his helmet up any day".

"Thank you kind sir", said J, ignoring Joycie's comment. "We've come for our tour".

A second policeman walked with them up a final winding road. In front of them towered Viceregal Lodge, an elaborate mock-Tudor building, surrounded by manicured gardens. The policeman handed The Six over to a Very Important Looking Man. He took them inside into a spacious lounge, which overlooked the gardens. A full cream tea was laid out on a large octagonal metal table.

"The Lord Irwin called to say you had spoken in church and that we should give you a special welcome", said The Very Important Looking Man.

"Who's he?" asked CA.

"Why young sir, he took over as the new Viceroy just yesterday. He is trying to foster a more open style of government, hence his invitation for you to visit. The Lord Irwin has offered his apologies but is travelling to Navjivan later today to meet with Mr Gandhi".

"Gosh", said CA.

They all sat down to take tea and were served by a team of waiters.

After tea, The Very Important Man showed them around the building: room upon room, filled with government workers, porters coming and going with boxes and trollies. Delhi was moving to Shimla for the summer!

"I was just thinking that my mother can only be about ten weeks old now", whispered CA. "This all feels very peculiar".

"Ah dear Mrs R", said J. "She always makes me a lovely tea before my elocution lesson. She is such a gifted Speech and Drama teacher".

After their grand tour, The Six decided to find Sham Lall & Sons to see Rupert's pictures. After a good long walk back down, they found it on The Mall, beneath Christ Church.

The Six entered the shop, which was full of old pictures and books. A very, very old man with a wispy beard approached them. J took a long look at him, feeling sure they had met before.

"How may I be of assistance young Sirs and Misses?" he asked.

"We would like to see Rupert Westover's pictures please", said Bog. "Would you be Mr Lall?"

"Oh no miss, Young Mr Lall is indisposed at the moment. I am Mr Lovegrove. Mr Rupert, yes of course. So sad that he passed away recently. Here are his pictures. I think this one is the finest. Apparently, he painted two almost identical pictures and his son Monty kept the other one".

The Six looked at the picture with open mouths. It was indeed almost identical to the one hanging in Bog's kitchen.

"I wish, I wish, I wish we were back home in Millington on Easter Sunday 1979", chanted J, touching the double six magic square clay tablet in her pocket.

A great wind whipped up, pictures flew out of their boxes and off the tables and once again, there were swirling lights. This time, there was the sound of a harp being played overhead. The Six held hands in a circle and felt their feet lifting off the ground. They were flying over the hills of Shimla, up and up towards the clouds.

After what seemed like an eternity of billowy white air, they felt themselves descending, down and down. They landed on the internal patio at Number Two, Bath Place, Millington just as Mrs Susan Cornwallis-West returned from her shopping expedition.

"Hello my darlings", she said. "Such a strange thing. I met this lovely old man on The Cobbles. He said his name was Mr Lovegrove and we had a fascinating conversation. He was in Shimla around the time I was born. There was something quite special about him. I think I need a whisky. Let's all have a drink!"

Yet again there was complete silence for a minute or two.

J put her hand into her left pocket and let out a cry:

"The double six magic square must have fallen out of my pocket as we ascended into the heavens".

Chapter 18. Party Time at Rooks Bend (Part Two)

A soothing cuppa later, Saturday 21st October 1978, Rooks Bend, Mellingford, Humbleshire

"I feel so much more relaxed", said Sheila. "Was that chamomile tea Jemima?"

"Let's just say it was a blend Mrs Rhodes".

Sheila got up from her beanbag and stumbled a little. She and Jemima walked around the house into the back garden, where the others were busily putting up the marquee.

Suddenly, there was a loud noise overhead. An aeroplane flew past and after a minute or two, CC shrieked:

"There's someone parachuting down!"

Indeed this was true and soon, the person hanging from the parachute seemed to be heading straight for them.

"This is very cool", said Sheila.

A man landed onto the rear lawns, removed his helmet, unfastened himself and let out a primal scream.

"Noel, it's you, I can't believe it", chirped Jemima.

"Greetings, fellow citizens of Humbleshire", boomed Noel. "Noel Hugo Timothy has entered the room! I've got a hard-on the size of Florida. Must be a full ten inches".

"Ye Gods!" uttered Bog. "I cannot believe how incredibly vulgar that is and by that I mean daddy would never talk about the size of his organ in public".

"Reminds me of Dawlish", mewed Sheila.

"I had five bowel movements this morning Mima and haven't shot my load in three days. It's going to be a night to remember".

Jemima reddened a little and rushed over to embrace Noel.

"Oh gosh, I see what you mean Nolly. I think your custard launcher is fully primed".

"Now then everyone", said J. "Enough of such frivolities. We have work to do. Let's get the marquee up and the sound stage ready. Mrs R, do you need help with the food and setting up the bar?"

"Really J it's all cool", said Sheila. "I ended up paying Mrs Hemstretch to do all the catering and CA's brother and his wife will be here soon to do the bar. Ian has already left. He's gone to stay with his friend Mr Whinny tonight so we can have a jolly good old boogy. I rather fancy another cup of tea".

"It'll be with you in a jiffy", said Jemima reassuringly. "Why don't you go inside and have a lie down? I'll bring it in".

"OK babe", said Sheila and wandered inside, humming "It's Not Unusual", her favourite Tom Jones song.

"Chaps, I have never seen mater this relaxed before. What have you done to her?" quizzed CA.

"I crumbled one of mummy's Valium into her tea", confessed Jemima.

"Well done Mima, you're a star. I thought I was going to get the ear bashing of my life when she met Julian".

"And why might that be pet?" asked Julian.

"Well she doesn't know about me if you know what I mean".

Julian rushed over to CA, threw his arms around him and gave him a big kiss, full on the lips.

"You may not have ten inches pet but you know what to do with what you've got".

"Enough", proclaimed J. "Right let's run the wiring into the house, set up the equipment and have a sound test".

It was another balmy autumn day and they all busied themselves with finishing off the marquee, laying out tables and chairs and rigging the fairy lights all around the garden as CC played DJ in the marquee.

"I had a dream last night", said J. "It was most queer. It was a dream about a dream that we Six are all going to have after we've knocked a wall down".

"Why didn't me and my Nolly have the dream?" asked Jemima.

"Or me?" asked Julian and Sandy in unison.

"My guides have not fully guided as me to why it was only we Six".

"I didn't know you were a guide J", said Noel. "Is it better to have a guide on your arm or a brownie in your trousers?"

"Oh that's awfully funny Nolly".

Jemima laughed so much, she had to briefly retire to her tent to effect a change of undergarment.

They all busied themselves until mid-afternoon, by which time Mrs Hemstretch had delivered a heaving sweet trolley and a huge cold buffet. This was laid out on the kitchen table under damp tea towels to keep the food fresh. CA's brother MJ and his wife Lilith had also arrived by then and set up the bar. MJ was under strict orders to monitor the flow of alcohol and only he had the key to the coal store, where extra supplies were held.

The other guests started to arrive from around five o'clock and by six, the front lawns were covered with colourful tents and teepees. The party wasn't actually due to start until seven.

"Come my love, let's retire for a while", said Noel to Jemima.

They wandered off to the front lawns, arm in arm and squeezed inside the tent.

"I have a bag full of freshly picked mushrooms", said Noel. "Interested?"

"What kind of mushrooms?" asked Jemima.

"The fun kind", said Noel.

"Oh Nolly, shall we have a little triplingtons?" said Jemima, sidling up to her beloved.

Noel poured out the contents of a large brown paper bag. They both took a little handful and started to munch on the mushrooms.

"They taste very earthy Nolly", said Jemima.

"Manna from heaven my darling. I think it's time I got my wanger out".

Chapter 19. Mrs Johnson's Psychedelic Gathering (Part Three)

Very slightly later, Friday 15th July 2022, Nutting Hill, Londinium

As the Ayahuasca began to take effect, The Six nestled into their beanbags. For a while, there was complete silence and then each of them saw the same, indistinct form hovering in the corner of the room.

J: Good evening Mr Lovegrove. I knew you would be with us.

B: You seem familiar. I feel from the very depths of my soul that I know you and by that I mean, we have encountered each other in another life.

CA: Every life.

T: I feel safe and warm.

CC: I can see a Great White Wall.

Joycie: I see it too. Let us walk together towards the wall.

Mr Lovegrove: Be brave my dears. Do not stray or hesitate.

J: I am the mortar between the bricks of the wall.

B: I am the vines growing up the wall.

CA: I am the whiteness of the wall.

T: I am the bricks.

CC: I am the foundations of the wall.

Joycie: I am the earth the foundations are built upon.

Mr Lovegrove: The wall must come down.

J: I am cracking the mortar between every brick.

B: My vines will grow into the cracks and break through them.

CA: I shall reflect the light of the sun and fire will come.

T: The fire will return the bricks to dust.

CC: The foundations will no longer support the wall.

Joycie: The earth will part from under the wall.

Mr Lovegrove: It is time.

There was a deafening crash and a blinding light, followed once again by complete silence and darkness for what seemed like hours. They all lay still and silent, their eyes closed.

Mr Lovegrove: Open your eyes and walk together.

J: I am the oceans, the rivers, lakes, waterfalls and rain. I am once again crystal clear and pure.

B: I am the air, the gentle breeze, no longer polluted by the ravages of man.

CA: I am the sun providing light and heat to wherever it is needed, never too much and always sufficient.

T: I am the earth, no longer tainted by waste and chemicals.

CC: I am the Plant Kingdom, feeding and healing the Animal Kingdom.

Joycie: I am the Animal Kingdom, always kind, honest, loving, respectful, hardworking and playful.

All together: We are the planet.

Mr Lovegrove: Your work is done. From henceforth, you will be the new guardians of life on Planet Earth. Now lie back and see the beauty of what you have saved.

Mrs Johnson, Bog, Christopher Anthony, Tdlz, Christopher Charles and Joycie snuggled into their beanbags and all had the same dream.

Chapter 20. Party Time at Rooks Bend (Part Three)

A few hours after Noel got his wanger out, Saturday 21st October 1978, Rooks Bend, Mellingford, Humbleshire

Tdlz Gdlpz-Goldfellow awoke with a start and scratched her head. She had just experienced the most vivid, rather apocalyptic dream, quite unlike any other she'd ever had before. (Being a woman who slept a lot, Tdlz had experienced many dreams throughout her seventeen and a half years).

"You've been out for an hour Tdlz", said J gently shaking her. "The party is well under way. Do come and have a boogie. Mrs R has been dancing around the garden and just shared a spliff with Bog".

Tdlz got up. She had fallen asleep on the bank at the end of the garden in the arms of a lepidopterist called Lavinia.

"I'm all tangled up", said Tdlz.

"Let me release you my little Swallowtail", said Lavinia. "There we go, fly away, fly away into the warm autumnal breeze".

"Thanks Lavvy", said Tdlz and got up very slowly.

The garden was bathed in fairy lights and CC was well into his second set of the night.

"Come and have a boogie Tdlz", repeated J sashaying towards the marquee.

Noel and Jemima were making strange chugging noises rather like a tugboat as Tdlz and J walked past them.

"I have delivered my cargo and am once more upon the open seas", boomed Noel.

"Landy ahoy Nolly. I'm so enjoying being a little ship and may I say your mast looks exceptionally well-polished".

Noel and Jemima continued to do circuits around the garden, tooting and making strange whooshing noises.

"I might ask CC to put on a bit of Demis Roussos to properly get us in the party mood", said J.

"Save your love my darling", interjected CA, sporting a new pair of blue corduroy dungarees as he tangoed though the ornamental garden towards them with Julian. "I shall be coming of age in twenty four minutes".

"Ohh pet, let's start a countdown to you coming", trilled Julian as he unzipped a layer of leather. "There you are Mrs Rhodes, there is flesh beneath the leather!"

Bog and Sheila were reclined on a large pile of floral cushions, watching a troupe of acrobats leaping over the badminton net.

"..and so Mrs Rhodes, that's the story of how mummy and daddy moved from Calcutta to Mellingford and by that I mean from Inja to Humbleshire", said Bog as she passed a reefer to Sheila.

"Fascinating babe", purred Sheila. "I always wanted to travel but Ian won't venture past Dorselshire. After I came of age, I spent a week in Dawlish with an exceptionally well endowed man called Montgomery. Would you be a darling and fetch me some nibbles please? I've got the munchies".

The rear gardens at Rooks Bend were a sight to see: there must have been around 100 young people dancing, singing, chanting poetry, meditating and generally having the time of their lives.

CA, J, Tdlz and Julian tangoed towards the marquee.

A young man who went by the name of Ashley Rummage approached them with one of Judy, the Spaniel's thick metal chain leads.

"Hey man, your parents are seriously progressive, I mean like openly sharing their love of bondage. It's so Seventies man".

"Give me my dog's lead you loon hippy", barked CA. "What on earth are you eating?"

"It's a Bonio man, I found it in a bag in your outside shed. It's like crunchy and so organic".

"That's dog food. For heaven's sake, get some proper food from the kitchen. I hear Mrs Hemstretch's avocado and shrimp vol-au-vents are a triumph".

"Hey man, chill. We're all creatures of The Universe. Vol-au-vents are like so bourgeois man. I'll stick with the Bonio".

CA, J, Tdlz and Julian entered the marquee, where CC was holding court behind two record decks, downing Malibu and pineapple with Joycie and wearing tartan clad headphones.

Everyone made their way into the tent as the hour approached midnight.

"Hold hands everyone, come on now let's get in a circle to wish CA a very Hippy Bothday", shouted J over Led Zeppelin.

The marquee was now filled with a sea of euphoric party goers, all chanting and singing, arm in arm.

"Ten, night, eight, seven, six, five, four, three, two, one..."

"And we're buying the stairway to heaven".

Chapter 21. The Dream (Part One)

Friday 15th July 2022, Everywhere and Nowhere

"I feel a bit peculiar", croaked J as she opened her eyes and tried to work out where she was. "I hope I didn't put too much garlic in the Ayahuasca".

"Me too", said Bog. "And by that I mean, I think my body is on a beanbag in Nutting Hill whilst my essence is wherever this is".

"I miss ma Kelvie", wailed CC. "I want to be twirled around ma bothy".

"I hope you have the right lubricant", chipped in CA.

"Wakey, wakey Tdlz", shrieked Joycie. "You should see this view".

"It can't be morning already", yawned Tdlz, trying to scratch a head she couldn't find. "Where's my head gone?"

"I think we're in the future", mused J. "Way up high, looking down on our planet. Let's relax and savour the beauty of what we have saved. Although we can't see each other, I can sense you all my darlings. It's so lovely being water-based, crystal-clear and lapis blue".

"How utterly breathtaking", gasped Bog. "I am literally the air and it's fresh and clean. Not a whiff of an emission and by that I mean neither carbon nor flatulence related".

"Now you come to mention it, I'm feeling very leafy, exceptionally rooted and fertile", whooped CC.

"I always said your fertility was wasted on the world Jerry", quipped CA, realising how pleasant it was being the sun.

"I really don't know whether to mew, bark, bray or whinny", chirped Joycie, embracing representation of the entire Animal Kingdom.

"Ancient civilisations have collapsed because they disregarded the care of their soil. Soil is our lifeline; it's fundamental to the health and well-being of our society, gives life to our food, cleans our air, filters and holds our water, and yes, even combats climate change. Compost feeds the soil that feeds us, let's feed her well", sermonised Tdlz.

"Gosh she wakes up quick", retorted J.

Suddenly there was a blinding flash of light, rather like when they were transported back to Shimla in 1979.

The Six felt themselves transforming back into their earthly bodies and were sucked into a swirling vortex, finally all landing onto an exceptionally large beanbag in the middle of an enormous billowy cloud.

A very tall old man with a long white beard was standing in front of them. He was dressed in a white linen suit and was sporting a white panama hat and a monocle.

"My dear children", he purred. "You have seen how your planet will heal. Now you must hear what is about to happen and what you must do to protect yourselves and those you love. Your world is about to change forever. The Nimbus Pandemic in 2020 was just the beginning".

"How lovely to see you Mr Lovegrove", trilled J.

Chapter 22. Party Time at Rooks Bend (Part Four)

Sunday 22nd October 1978, Rooks Bend, Mellingford, Humbleshire

"Christopher Anthony Rhodes, wake up immediately. Your father is due back this evening and Rooks Bend looks like a bomb's hit it. I just saw someone spending tuppence behind the oak tree at the bottom of the garden. I think it was Noel Timothy but I've never seen him from that angle before. This is all really upsetting. Oh yes, Happy Birthday. In theory, you're a man now but there's little evidence to show it".

Sheila Rhodes was not feeling her best. After partying into the small hours and consuming a bottle of tequila, she woke in the middle of the night and vomited over Judy the Spaniel.

"Mrs R, I can assure you that your son was as much a man yesterday as he is today".

Julian peeked his head out from under the eiderdown in CA's bedroom.

"Hell's teeth, this just gets worse and worse", howled Sheila. "Get up and come downstairs right now. This mess needs clearing up".

"Message received and understood mater".

CA and Julian got up and staggered down to the kitchen where a large number of the previous night's party goers were consuming coffee and toast.

"I think you need another cup of my tea Mrs R", said Jemima. "You look like you need soothing. If I might say so, you were exceptionally game last night".

"Thank you my dear. That would be most acceptable".

"I'm back Mima. That was the best movement I think I've ever had. I found a rather large brassiere hanging from the hammock. Who can it belong to?" beamed Noel.

"Like I said last night, your parents are seriously progressive", croaked Ashley Rummage, drawing on a foot long reefer.

"Here you are Mrs R, drink this tea. You'll be as right as nine pence before you know it. I've made it a little stronger than yesterday's".

"Thank you my dear", said Sheila taking a sip. "Gosh, it tastes of honey and cinnamon and there's a strange after taste".

CA's brother MJ and his wife Lilith had got up around seven and had been busying themselves with starting to clear up the mess. Tdlz, being an early-riser had been helping them along with J and Sandy.

"All hands to the pump", commanded J. "If we all pull together, this can be sorted in no time at all".

Judy the spaniel ran into the kitchen, barking and making a fuss of everyone.

"I thought she was an Apricot Roan", said Bog, who had just returned from the cabbage field at the bottom of the garden after a two hour meditation with Joycie. "Her colouring is altogether different today and by that I mean strangely speckled".

"Come Judy", said Sheila. "Come to mumsy, it's time for a shampoosy-woosy. You must give me the recipe for that tea Jemima. I feel so much calmer now".

"I was a ship last night everyone, honest I was", said Joycie. "The back garden was the sea and I was a ship. It was quite a voyage. I was part of a fleet with Mima and Noel".

Suddenly there was a loud wheezing and groaning sound. CC and Kelvin marched into the kitchen, once again in full Highland Dress, each with a set of bagpipes.

"Cripes, it's Moira Anderson and Kenneth McKellar in personae", uttered J.

CC and Kelvie performed a five minute Highland Fling, followed by a rousing version of "Donald Where's Your Troosers" on the bagpipes.

There followed an appreciative round of applause from everyone.

"Right", said J. "Let's get this party finished. Everyone take a bin bag and comb the place, inside and out. All glasses, cutlery and crockery to the kitchen. CA and I will be washing up. The Millington Sail and Tent Company have just pulled up to de-erect the marquee".

"Sometimes I wish you could de-erect my darling", said Jemima.

"Let's go and clear out our tent first babe", boomed Noel. "There's enough custard ready for a trifle the size of Humbleshire".

They all pulled together and by around five in the afternoon, everything had been cleared up. All the guests had left apart from The Six, who were sitting in a circle in the paddock on a groundsheet.

"I had one of my predictive dreams last night", said J. "It was quite alarming in some ways but ultimately very reassuring. I won't trouble you with the details right now but be prepared for a Big Journey starting in 2022".

"Were we all in it?" asked CA.

"Very much so", said J.

Chapter 23. The Dream (Part Two)

Friday 15th July 2022, on an enormous billowy cloud

"It is a pleasure and a privilege to see you too my dear Mrs Johnson", said Mr Lovegrove. "You have done well".

"Excuse me, excuse me my good man and by that I am directing this to you there in the white suit. I am feeling alarmed, my plunging breasts are sensitive to the touch and I know that means I am in flight mode. I'm not feeling at all safe on this enormous billowy cloud", snarled Bog.

"Don't speak to Mr Lovegrove like that Boggy", he's the main man if you know what I mean", hissed J.

"Main man, main man? He looks like he's just stepped out of a Barbara Cartland novel, not that I have ever read any Barbara Cartland novels but my sister Crinoline is addicted and by that I mean, she has an insatiable hunger for romance and exotic men".

"Like ma Kelvie", swooned CC. "I like this cloud".

"Wake up Tdlz", said Joycie. "You're out for the count again".

"I was having such a nice dream".

CA stood up, took a deep breath and uttered:

"Take this kiss upon the brow!
And, in parting from you now,
Thus much let me avow-
You are not wrong, who deem

That my days have been a dream;
Yet if hope has flown away
In a night or in a day,
In a vision, or in none,
Is it therefore the less gone?
Is but a dream within a dream.

I stand amid the roar
Of a surf-tormented shore,
And I hold within my hand
Grains of the golden sand-
How few! yet how they creep
Through my fingers to the deep,
While I weep-while I weep!
Oh God! can I not grasp
Them with a tighter clasp?
Oh God! can I not save
One from the pitiless wave?
Is all that we see or seem
But a dream within a dream?"

"Oh CA, that was lovely", said J. "Word perfect. A Dream
Within A Dream' by Edgar Allen Poe, one of my favourite
pomes".

"My favourite ex-client used to pay me a grand every
month to recite it while she bathed in asses' milk",
reminisced CA.

"You've ruined it now", said J.

"My dears, please calm down and focus", said Mr
Lovegrove. "I know this is a lot for you all to take in. You
have created a future for The Human Race but there is a
long and tortuous road yet to travel before you can truly

settle. There will be earthquakes, plagues, financial collapse, digital eclipse; many will perish. Mother Gaia has decreed that The Change must happen like this now. Your people did not listen to Her Words: Kindness, Honesty, Love and Respect. She sent so many signs: the storms and Nimbus Virus of 2020 were her final warning. And yet, your people went back to their former ways just when they had a chance to heal their world".

Everyone started to cry, their tears flowing down upon the billowy cloud into little iridescent pools.

"How could we let this happen?" sobbed J. "Our beautiful planet has to suffer so much more before we can find our peace. What must we do now Mr Lovegrove?"

"You have eighteen months from today to come together. You must come together. You must be together with those you love the most. You must all leave your homes and relocate to Millington Lodge in Humbleshire. Collectively you and your loved ones can make this happen. When you moved there Tdlz, you did not know that it is the central energy seat in your world".

"Who'd have thought it?" gasped Tdlz.

"My dears, have you heard me well?"

There was a resounding "yes" and for the fourth time in their lives, the swirling lights returned and they found themselves floating gently down into their individual beanbags at J's flat in Nutting Hill, Londinium.

One by one, they awoke from the same dream and for some time there was complete silence.

"You must all go now my darlings", whispered J.

"We shall meet again on Monday 15th January 2024 at Millington Lodge".

Chapter 24. Joycie's Homecoming

"Bye bye Boggy", chirped Joycie as Bog got out of the Phantom and skipped towards her luxury mobile home.

"I am home my darling Vladdie and by that I mean I am returned and we have a lot to talk about. The world as we know it is about to change forever. I have missed your tender embraces. My plunging breasts were briefly sensitive to the touch yesterday during a vision we all shared but now they are once more soft and ready for your sweet lips".

"Darlink, you must to the bedroom now so I can to welcome you back in the way most deservink for my returnink moondust".

And with that, Bog was gone, leaving a faint scent of jasmine hanging in the air.

"I better get a welcome like that from my Clinton when we get home or there'll be hell to pay", hissed Joycie.

CC had flown back from Londinium to Edlingtonburgh. Kelvin would be collecting him from the airport in their lilac Mini Cooper with his familiar, Lasher the Chihuahua. It was then a two hour drive back to their bothy in Gussette-on-Spey.

"Parker, could you please activate the filters on the windows?" asked Tdlz. "I'm not in the mood for adulation today".

"Yus milday".

The Phantom wove its way through the country lanes of The Old Forest and soon they were on the outskirts of Millington where Joycie lived with her family. They pulled into Lawn Gardens and glided to a halt outside number 69.

"Tdlz, I can't thank you enough. This has been a life changing weekend. There are parts I can't remember but I know what we have to do and will get a plan in action soonest. Parker thank you for bringing us safely home".

"My pleasure Mrs Wort".

Joycie got out of the Phantom and a small crowd had already gathered, including a reporter from The Millington Advertiser.

"Mrs Wort, have you been somewhere special with Millington's First Lady?" asked Brian Brent, gossip columnist from The Advertiser.

"We went to see a friend in Londinium and had a super time. I met Jane McDonald and went to a drag show in So Ho Ho".

"Joycie, I would be sparing with details", whispered Tdlz. "I think we need to keep all this under wraps for now. Parker, to Millington Lodge".

The Phantom sped off and Joycie fought her way through an ever growing crowd of onlookers, let herself in through the side gate, locked it fast behind her and went into the kitchen via the back door.

"Mum, it's you!" her oldest child Chardonnay cried out, frantically stirring a large pot of stew. "You're still almost completely unrecognisable apart from the birthmark on your left thigh that looks like a strawberry. Our Kevin is out with his friends, most likely shoplifting and our Sharon is upstairs. She locked herself in her room on Thursday and hasn't been out since. The upstairs landing reeks of doobie and she's been chanting a lot and playing Gong. Dad's been leaving food and drink outside her door and emptying a potty twice a day. I've been working my fingers to the bone. Please don't ever go away again".

"You are my rock as ever Char. Where is dad?" asked Joycie.

"Dad is upstairs ironing. He's expecting you".

"Clinton Wort, come down here immediately", commanded Joycie. "No uniform required, we need to talk, NOW!"

Clinton rushed down the stairs. He hadn't shaved in four days, was wearing a soiled vest and a pair of ripped Y-Fronts.

"Clinton Wort, you look like a Beverly Hillbilly. I've been away two days and this is the kind of homecoming I get. Bog's husband was waiting at the door for her, full of romantic intentions and I get son shoplifting, daughter self-incarcerating and husband in soiled undergarments".

"I wasn't expecting you until six Joycie. I had to work three double shifts in a row and only got back an hour ago. I've been worried senseless. You never called and I was imagining you were getting up to all kinds of mischief with those debauched friends. I was about to shower off the flock then iron my uniform".

"Well yes, the roads were very clear and we left early. I'm sorry I didn't call, there just wasn't time. We need to sit down and talk. There have been some very significant developments. There's no easy way to say this. We have eighteen months to move out of here and re-locate to Millington Lodge".

Clinton's jaw dropped and he went very pale.

"Did you hear me Clinton? We must talk. Go and shower then meet me in the garden chalet at six. I need a Malibu and pineapple to help me settle while I wait for you".

"Yes dear".

Chapter 25. Two Hander in The Cairngorms

Sunday 17th July, 2022, Gussette-on-Spey, Abercrombieshire

"Wakey, wakey Christopher Charles, it's a beautiful summer's day and we need to be oot there romping in the heather!"

Kelvin gave CC a firm nudge. It was past noon and he was still fast asleep.

"Not now Kelvie, I'm spent. Och no, Lasher get off ma scrotal sack. I herniated a testicle in 1979 and they've not been for nibbling on ever since".

"Christopher Charles, we need to talk. You made no sense last night. All that talk about the world coming to an end unless we relocate to Millington. I know we had a move planned but living in a commune with your sassenach friends is stretching it".

"But we had a vision Kelvie. It was real. We drank soup and it had things in it and we all had a dream. I was all the trees and flowers. We were on an enormous billowy cloud and an old man dressed in white told us what we had to do. We have to move to Millington Lodge by 15th January 2024 to save the world".

"Christopher Charles, you have always been prone to hyperbole but this really is the limit. Get yourself up, shower and we'll go for a wee ramble".

CC got out of bed and limped into their Roman mosaic shower room. He selected a range of products, turned the water on and started to sing in his rich, deep baritone voice:

"I dreamed a dream in times gone by
When hope was high and life worth living
I dreamed, that love would never die
I dreamed that God would be forgiving
Then I was young and unafraid
And dreams were made and used and wasted
There was no ransom to be paid
No song unsung, no wine untasted"

CC lathered himself, thinking of Susan Boyle and wishing she were there to guide him in his time of inner torment.

"I had a dream my life would be
So different from this hell I'm living
So different now from what it seemed
Now life has killed the dream
I dreamed"

"Och you're not having a Susan meltdown are you pet"? quizzed Kelvin. "You only sing Susan when you're having one of your episodes".

CC got out of the shower, specially adapted to cater for his six foot nine stature. He started to towel his long black locks, sobbing gently.

"I've seen it predicted in the stars Kelvie. You know I'm never wrong. Ma Patrick Moore may have been gone nearly ten years now, but his spirit lives. When I look up to the sky at night, I sometimes think I can see him sitting astride The Plough. I tell you Kelvie, I saw this coming before I went to Londinium and I warned you then. It's for real now".

"Christopher Charles, put on your three piece plaid rambling suit and get yourself outside with me. We need to connect with nature and talk this through".

CC dabbed his eyes, got dressed and went into the kitchen to make himself a bowl of porridge and a cup of his favourite vanilla latte. Kelvin came and sat next to him, massaging his broad shoulders.

"You're well and truly knotted Christopher Charles. What did you get up to in Londinium? You've got yourself all tizzed up".

"Och Kelvie, that's bliss. Where would I be without you? I thank Susan for the day I saw you heaving that enormous caber back in 1977".

"That was 45 years ago today sweetheart".

"Och no, I forgot. How can you forgive me Kelvie? I've been too caught up in the perils of saving our world. How can I make it up to you?"

"Sing with me Ceecy. Something cheerier than Susan".

CC stood up, narrowly missing his head on an oak beam and cleared his throat. Kelvin stood in front of him, his eyes fixed upon CC.

CC: Sometimes it's hard to be a ma-an
K: Boom da boom da boom
CC: Giving all your love to just one man.
K: Ah, ah, ah, boom
CC: You'll have bad times
K: Boom, boom, boom

CC: And he'll have good times, doin' things that you don't understand.
K: Ah, boom, ah boom
CC: But if you love him, you'll forgive him, even though he's hard to understand.
KK: Ah, ah, ah, boom
CC: And if you love him, oh be proud of him, 'cause after all he's just a man

CC and Kelvie embraced, the tears flowing and with Lasher howling in the background, sang a rousing chorus in unison:

"Stand By Your Man,
Give him two arms to cling to,
And someone warm to come on
When nights are cold and lonely.
Stand By Your Man,
And tell the world you love him,
Giving all the love you can.
Stand By Your Man".

"I will move to Millington Lodge with you Ceecy. I will. You are my man and I am your man and together we will help to save the world as men".

"I'll get straight onto Mistress Niven from Scottish House Move first thing tomorrow Kelvie. I can feel it in ma bones: we'll be celebrating next Hogmanay in Millington".

Chapter 26. For Sale, Luxury Mobile Home

Tuesday 16th August 2022, Fartlebrook, Humbleshire

"No you can't come with us Crinoline and by that I mean the offer is only open to me and to Vladimir".

"Mummy would not approve Lou. This is not ethically acceptable from a familial perspective. It flies in the face of everything we were brought up to cherish as a given. You are inviting the very worst kind of karma into your future and I am beyond devastated".

"Tough".

Bog slammed the phone down on her sister, drew deeply on a Sobrani and gulped back a third glass of Campari.

"Vladdie, this is all getting rather nasty. Praline is no longer talking to me and after that conversation, I think we can kiss goodbye to Crin too. Only Aunt Yootha understands. I would have asked her to come with but at 93, she said it would all be too much for her".

"My darlink, come to your Vladimir. I shall whisper into your delicate ear hole and soothe you", purred Vladimir, recently returned from an all night sky-watching session with The Sandy Balls Gazers.

"You are all I need my darling and by that I mean every cell in my heavenly body is aligned with every cell in your heavenly body. I am Romulus to your Remus, Castor to your Pollux".

"Is like Sugar and Testicle darlink"?

"Castor see Polux sunt stelele 'gemeeeny cerestee' care da erm numele lor constelatei Gemenilore"

"Ah yes I see. Your Romanian is coming along very beautifully my darlink. We are two Weasleys, connected with magical threads between our solar plexuses. It was written in the skies that we would connect and be absolutely super dooperly happy together".

"And so the paradise we built is finally up for sale Vladdie. I thought we would end our days together here, interlocked in embrace as we breathed our last breaths simultaneously. It is not meant to be and by that I mean I shall connect with my "inner Jane" and embrace a gritty realism in the way I approach the coming months. I may even adopt a Northern accent from time to time to enhance my new reality".

"I think the Sandy Balls Gazers may put in an offer in the very soon my sveetyheart. They are wanting to take it on as their observatory".

Bog filled her glass and fixed her gaze upon Vladimir.

"Ey up and Ecky thump Vladimir. There's nowt better than that. I'll allus love you, It'll be reight good".

"I am not understandink your labial speakings".

"My darling, between the two of us, your language is always the language of love. There are certain things you should possibly avoid saying in public. By that I mean 'labial' is a bit iffy".

"But you know how I love to gently kiss your always invitink labia".

"Lips, Vladimir, lips. Anything labia-related must remain strictly entre nous. Do you understand? Like the character from that delightfully proletarian play by Mike Leigh, I look into my mirror and tell myself every morning how beautiful my lips are. I am feeling strangely retro today and have a hunger. Could I tempt you to a cheesy pineapple?"

"That would be super doper draga mea. Let us go to our love chamber in this very moment".

Chapter 27. Much Ado in Millington (Part One)

Friday 5th January 2024, Millington Lodge, Humbleshire

I'm rushed off my feet. Finalising 42 redundancy packages and converting the lodge into six units has been a tall order. These people are my family. I must do the right thing by them all. So much change so quickly. Someone called me "Mrs Churchill" the other day. I rather like that.

Wilma get down. You are not allowed on the chaise-longue. Don't look at me like that and stop drooling. Here have your favourite toy, no not mummy's bicep expanders. Put them down. NOW!

And so readers, it falls upon my broad shoulders, Mrs Tdlz Sharon Gdlpz-Goldfellow (MBE), Monklands Comprehensive Sportswoman of the Year 1976, to share with you all the extraordinary changes that are escalating by the day.

Nearly eighteen months have passed since we got together in Londinium. Initially, I was somewhat sceptical about the predictions. However, over the last six months, it has become increasingly clear that the global order (such as it was) has changed forever.

The 2020 Nimbus Pandemic was just the beginning; a warning of things to come. After 6 months of social isolation, we were able to start picking up the pieces again and returned to a "new normal" by late 2020. The UK death toll was worse than feared at the start of the virus, mainly affecting the more vulnerable in society. I shall never forget the leaked footage of Mr Johnson rubbing his hands in glee saying "tidy end to the social care crisis".

All cinemas and about half of pubs open at the beginning of the virus closed forever along with multiple small and larger businesses. It's even more about streaming and social media now and people don't go out so much. All of the population are supported under the new National Assistance Programme in some shape, sense or form now. We were hopeful that something new and positive would emerge from all the losses we suffered but by mid-2022, too many things had returned to the way they had been before the Nimbus Pandemic.

People just never learn.

The San Francisco and Tokyo earthquakes within a week of each other were the first real signs that the planet's anger was on the ascendant. That was in July 2023. The combined death toll was in excess of five million. Both cities were devastated. Stock markets crashed and never recovered. People began to barter as the concept of currency was losing all meaning. Fortunately, I cashed in my many investment chips in August 2022 and instead, purchased gold and platinum.

The Cumulo-Nimbus Pandemic really started to bite in September 2023. It was thought to have been initially contained within Moscow but soon spread globally. The death toll to date is reported to be in excess of a billion. Unprecedented levels of civil unrest continue to be reported globally. To say that the world is in a state of pure unbridled panic would be an understatement.

The Cumulo-Nimbus Pandemic spread like a tidal wave, strangely affecting the rich more than the poor. King William V now sits on the throne, a lonely childless widower and a grey shadow of his former self. Prince

Harry is heir apparent, though he and Megan have been reported as siding with the ever growing Republican Movement since returning to the United Kingdom.

Wilma, GET DOWN! Oh what the hell. Stay up. It really doesn't matter anymore. I need to get used to having mud on my fabrics.

Chapter 28. Three Hander in a Removal Van

Sunday 14th January 2024, en route to Millington ex Londinium

After over a year, Mrs Johnson and CA were eventually able to barter their properties to a wealthy half Puerto Rican, half American Injan ex client of CA's called Gina Crow Shoe.

Gina had worked for the United Nations for many years and whenever she was in Londinium, she would hire CA to recite poetry to her while she bathed in asses' milk. Although life in Londinium had become increasingly perilous, Gina's connection with CA was so strong that she decided to take on both Nutting Hill properties. As cash had lost all value by the time the transaction neared completion, Gina managed to negotiate a complex package of goods, which were delivered to Millington Lodge.

The removal van had pulled up outside CA and J's properties late afternoon on Friday 12th January and they hit the road just before midnight. J's long-term secret lover, Mr Hogle had moved in with her a little more than a year previously and was travelling with J and CA to Millington Lodge in the back of the van. Once all their belongings had been loaded into the van, CA and Mr Hogle set up a cosy corner for the three of them with adequate supplies of alcohol, food and toiletries. They also had a Sanilav that J's former employer Betsit had given her, before she closed her bakery. A heap of hay bales served as seats.

Mr Hogle's twin siblings Telstar and Hendrick were at the wheel and had welded the tailgate to fortify it after J, CA and Mr Hogle had got inside. They knew not how long it would be, if ever before they would reach their destination and that until then, they would only have each other for company.

It had taken them nearly two days to reach the outskirts of Londinium, following the recent city-wide riots. Telstar and Hendrick had been fully briefed by Gina Crow Shoe, who was well connected across the Londinium Network. The van was held in an encampment at Humpington Court Palace for nearly 24 hours until Telstar made contact with Gina Crow Shoe. She managed to intervene by trading 100 gallons of asses' milk for their release.

Finally, just after dusk on Sunday 14th January, they were able to move onto quieter country lanes and hoped for a smoother final leg.

CA: We must have been in the back of this effin contraption for nigh on two days . There's only one torch between the three of us and it's making bowel movements a rather tricky manoeuvre. I have no idea where we are or where we're going. It's been stop, start, stops lasting hours, start, stop. We're in a vacuum. Care for another bottle of Guinless Mr Hogle?

H: To be sure I would. May the little folk dance around your feet.

J: Boys, you're on your fourth crate. Try switching to chamomile tea? It's very soothy.

H: May the road rise up to meet you Mrs Johnson. That's an arseways and quare thing to suggest, to be sure.

CA: You're not wrong Mr H. I've lost my mood ring and don't know how I feel about that.

H: And the Lord said unto John, "Come forth and you will receive eternal life".

CA: But John came fifth and won a toaster.

CA and H both fell off their respective hay bales, laughed like drains and managed to break wind together in perfect unison.

J: Vacuums do not smell of the very worst kind of flatus boys. In all my born days I have not had to endure such disgustingness.

H: I read in the Dublington Times that Mr Eammon Penis is changing his name to Patrick.

CA: My family has a genetic predisposition for diarrhoea. It runs in our jeans.

H: I have a stepladder because my real ladder left when I was a kid.

CA: What do you call a magic dog? A Labracadabrador.

J: Boys, please stop the hilarity. I think we're travelling down the Belinus Line, named after King Belinus who ruled and built roads from 380-363 BC. The Belinus Line is the father and mother of all ley lines, crossing the country from north to south like a spine.

H: You are a very wise Mrs Johnson. Experience is the comb that life gives to a bald man.

CA: It's a lonely wash that has no man's shirt in it.

H: God's help is nearer than the door.

114

J: Please, please can we be serious? You cannot rely on alcohol to lubricate each and every rusty cog in the great combine harvester we call life.

H: An old broom knows the dirty corners best.

There was a long silence and after a while, they all fell into deep and much needed slumbers. The removal van sped through the countryside towards Millington. Telstar and Hendrick stopped for a long rest break near Windchestington after so many hours of travelling.

By late morning, they pulled up outside Millington Lodge. Telstar and Hendrick got out the welding torch and started to unseal the tailgate.

"CA, I've been meaning to ask you for years what is in that rather large old leather portmanteau?" quizzed J, pointing to said item.

"That's my father's suitcase", said CA. "I'm going to open it up one day soon and write a book about everything that's in it".

Chapter 29. Much Ado in Millington (Part Two)

Monday 15ᵗʰ January 2024, Millington Lodge, Humbleshire

Hello there, it's "Mrs Churchill" again!

A huge storm is predicted next month. Nobody seems to know when and what may happen. Thankfully, the conversion work to Millington Lodge is as good as done and to say we've had it fortified would be an understatement.

We're having a bit of a do this evening as CA, J and Hogle moved in today. We're all finally together under one roof.

Well it's all go here. The removal van arrived from Londinium late morning. How our hearts sang when Telstar and Hendrick un-welded the tailgate. J, Hogle and CA emerged, blinking in the sunlight after so many hours inside the removal van. Telstar and Hendrick got back on the road pretty quickly as they have more removals to cover in the coming days.

J looked stylish in a turquoise roll-neck top and contrasting peach linen culottes, her blond hair glistening in the winter sun. Hogle was sporting a cream safari suit, his jet black hair slicked back. J is still married to Jonas Johnson but contact has been all but lost. Hogle moved into J's flat late July 2022 ending years of clandestine encounters. CA looked like he had recently emerged from the undergrowth, wisps of straw poking out from his blue corduroy dungarees.

J burst into tears and fell upon Hogle's shoulder. Life in the capital has been harsh these last few months. It took them a long time to get a good barter for their properties. People have been flocking out of the cities but they held out and got a good deal. We'll have sufficient water, gas, dry and tinned goods, petroleum, candles, beer and wine to last several years. The restored barn is full and under double lock and key!

CC and Kelvin were the first to move in. Their boutique croft sold within a week back in August 2022 and they lived in a caravan in the paddock until their unit was completed. The proceeds of their sale financed all the construction work including insulation, double glazing, flood defence, earthquake-proofing and four walk-in wardrobes for CC.

Bog and Vlad came shortly afterwards in time for Christmas 2022. They too sold their property in Fartlebrook before The Big Crash and with Bog's ever astute financial prowess, they purchased 100 acres of good arable land right next to Millington Lodge with enough trees to provide all the wood we'll ever need. Vlad purchased and installed our solar powered heating system. They have already been planting new saplings. Bog is Sustainability Personified and by that I mean she is worth her weight in gold!

Joycie and Clinton arrived in time for Christmas 2023. After The Big Crash, they decided not to sell their property. It's only a ten minute walk from Millington Lodge so it will be useful to have as a space for visitors. They have converted much of it into workshops, therapy spaces and a big kitchen. It's becoming a real community barter hub known as "Lentune Works" and is co-managed by Chardonnay, Sharon and Kevin. Clinton and Joycie co-designed and financed the new communal/kitchen areas

117

and underfloor heating at Millington Lodge. Joycie is mother to us all, never far from her kitchen and her beloved postman!

The World Wide Web is no more. There had been an increasing number of outages throughout 2023; a fatal virus finally did its work and all our screens are now blank. The Digital Age is over and good riddance say I! We have three generators and CA has brought his vinyl, sound system and precious I-Pod, gifted to him by Yours Truly for his fiftieth. CC brought all his CDs and DVDs. With J's Bontempi organ and Bog's flute, we'll never go short on musical entertainment!

CA is actively involved in "The Words" movement. It's all part of a new way of being, or rather returning to old ways. Gatherings are informal, almost a new form of local government. The "Foundation Pillars" are: "Kindness, Honesty, Love and Respect". I thought it was all a bit Hippy Dippy at first but now realise that these are the cornerstones of a civilised society and will bind us together.

Just a moment, someone's at the door. I'll be back in a mo....

.....sorry about that, it was Martina and Sue, dropping off a crate of Bollinger. How very thoughtful they are.

I struggle to believe that two of my icons (I so loved Wimbledon and Bake Off) are now part of my inner circle of friends. Both their partners were taken by the Cumulo-Nimbus Pandemic. They met at a women only spa in Bridlington, where they'd both gone to regroup. They decided to embark on a tour of England and extraordinarily, ended up buying "Rooks Bend" in Mellingford, where CA and his family had lived from 1970 until he sold it in 1997.

I met them at a local sporting event and we're firm friends now.

And so the party has begun. We're eleven for dinner tonight, including Wilma. Finally, we're all together. It's been tough the last six months and there will be tougher times ahead.

As I sit here sipping my Drambuie, I feel very blessed to be surrounded by my family.

There is one person missing tonight but she'll always be with us.

We decided to rename Millington Lodge and Vlad finished off the beautiful new sign today.

"Glynnis Meadows".

Chapter 30. The Epilogue

Tuesday 15ᵗʰ July 2047, Glynnis Meadows, Millington, Humbleshire

Tdlz and CA whistled a merry tune in unison as they cycled along the winding lanes of Millington. They turned into the rather overgrown gravel driveway of what once was Millington Lodge and raced each other, avoiding the potholes and overgrown shrubbery.

"Joycie and Clinton have been hard at it all day. There's enough food to feed the five thousand. Pass me some string please Mr Hogle", sang J as she wove garlands of daisies around the communal entrance.

After Jonas Johnson perished in The Great Fire of 2025, J married her secret childhood sweetheart. She met Mr Hogle at a Londinium gig in 1979. This was a few months after her previous partner Sandy had run off with a Lithuanian pole dancer.

"Consider it done my love. I've been out sawing wood for the stove and fire all day. Who needs gas and electricity?" eulogised Hogle.

"We managed without gas electricity AND 'Loose Women' for millennia and by that I mean almost the entire history of the planet. I miss them not and love our new life together with every inch of my human form. Vladdie my love, tonight the moon will be as full as my heart is for your most tender embraces. Have you settled the horses?" quizzed Bog as she scrubbed the front steps.

"Darlink they seem to settle themselves nowadays. I have been putting the finishing touches to our lovely new observatory", announced Vlad as he cleaned the downstairs windows.

"Clinton, where are you? I'm waiting. The baking is done but the oven is still hot. Scullery now!" commanded Joycie from the kitchen window.

"No my darling. Not now, later. Patience is a virtue", asserted Clinton as he ironed a brand new postman's uniform.

"Hen, I canna find the black hair dye", came a voice from deep within the ground floor annexe".

"Christopher Charles. How many times do I have to tell you, grey is the new black", growled Kelvin, arranging a sea of candles around the rear entrance.

Out of nowhere came a whirring and buzzing sound like an old car starting, followed by a loud burst of music from the marquee on the front lawn.

"Result", boomed CA. "I got that old generator working after all these years. Reckon there's enough petrol to give us a whole night of music. That I-Pod you gave me for my 50th Tdlz is still working and has all the tunes a party could ask for. My sound system is as ever, pukka".

CA is "ecstatically single", having taken a lifelong vow of celibacy on Saturday 16th July 2022. These days, he describes himself as "more of a kundalini and cocoa man".

The Six and their loved ones are all well into their eighties now but you wouldn't think it. They have managed their journey well together but the early years were challenging. One of the plagues nearly took CA and Tdlz but with round the clock care from their loved ones, they pulled through. They lost electricity during The Great Six Day Storm of 2024 and parts of the old lodge were destroyed. They supported each other through every disaster according to The Words.

Today is the 25th anniversary of The Day Things Changed. Today, The Six and their loved ones are throwing a party for their families and the former surviving staff of Millington Lodge.

The changes were not immediate, happening at first slowly over a period of some years from July 15th 2022; cities crumbled, governments fell and stock markets crashed. Barter became the new global currency. There were floods, earthquakes, fires, storms and plagues. Sixty percent of the population of Planet Earth in 2022 has now perished. All things digital and nuclear have ceased to be. Zero Carbon Footprint has been embraced.

The guests started to arrive. The wine flowed fast and free and trestle tables were laden high with Joycie's fine fare. The music played and everyone sang and danced until the early hours.

CA's brother MJ (now a sprightly 96) and his wife Lillith travelled from their home in Dorselshire to join the party. Their sons Matto and Jello joined them along with wives, Elkie and Lilkie.

J's son Speet, his wife Biddy, and their children Miles and Donna played "What's In My Cupboard" with CA, Kelvin and CC (his outfit, a symphony in blue complimenting shoulder length jet black locks).

Joycie and Clinton danced the tango as Bog played "Mi Buenos Aires Querido" on her flute, accompanied by J on her Bontempi organ with Chardonnay, Sharon and Kevin on percussion.

Tdlz finally finished a 500,000 piece jigsaw puzzle of Antarctica.

Mrs Johnson and CA sat on two beanbags on the front steps of Glynnis Meadows watching the sun rise over another bright new day. There was a sudden gust of wind and six white feathers fluttered down and fell at their feet, one by one.

Mrs Johnson looked up to the heavens, stroked the double six magic square hanging around her neck, smiled serenely and gently whispered:

"Thank you Mr Lovegrove".

Christopher Anthony Rhodes was born in 1960 and grew up in a small village sounding a bit like Mellingford in a county sounding a bit like Humbleshire.

After graduating from The University of The White Knights, Professor Rhodes enjoyed a long and varied career, initially in the film industry and latterly in health and social care settings. Numerous sabbaticals enabled him to travel extensively. At times, he may have touched upon the world of international male escorts in a city sounding a bit like Londinium.

Professor Rhodes now lives in semi-retirement somewhere like
The Green Island, (a favourite haunt of The Six).

Professor Rhodes thanks Ronaldo Augusto de Melo Niemeyer
for creating the cover art to this book along with Mrs Johnson and Mrs Ceausescu,
who at crucial times acted as his muses.

"Mrs Johnson's Psychedelic Gathering" was conceived on Thursday
23rd November 2017 in the middle of a heatwave in Goa, Inja.
To read more please visit Professor Rhodes' blog:

http://journeying-man.blogspot.com/

Coming Soon:"**My Father's Suitcase**"
On 16th July 2024 after a chance encounter with
Mr Lovegrove, CA decides to open his father's
suitcase. Join him on an epic journey, spanning
seven centuries and nearly as many continents.

Printed in Great Britain
by Amazon

41553705R00076